PRIDE & PREJUDICE
PETITE 1 TALES

# A FINE STOUT Love

*and other stories*

# Renée Beyea

Published by **Oakham Press**
an imprint of Renée Beyea
www.reneebeyea.com

Publisher's Note: This is a work of fiction. Names, characters, places, and incidents are inspired by Jane Austen or are a product of the author's imagination. Locales and public names are sometimes used for atmospheric purposes. Any resemblance to actual people, living or dead, or to businesses, companies, events, institutions, or locales is completely coincidental.

Cover photos from Novel Expression and Shutterstock
Cover Design by Roseanna White Designs
Book Layout © 2014 BookDesignTemplates.com

Unless otherwise identified, Scripture quotations are from the King James Version of the Bible.

**A Fine Stout Love and Other Stories/ Renée Beyea**. — 1st ed.
ISBN-13: 978-1-944224-00-4 Paperback
ISBN-13: 978-1-944224-01-1 Kindle
ISBN-13: 978-1-944224-02-8 EPUB

Version: 151218P

In Loving Memory

# Karisa L. Bennett

sister of my heart,
true friend and
incurable romantic

# CONTENTS

-------------------------------------------------------------

# PREFACE

*A word about organization…*

The stories in this collection are organized for suggested reading pleasure. However, they are not sequential and may be read in any order. The afterword includes a sentence synopsis of each as well as insight into their inspiration. Fine-print notations near the title headings orient each story within the chronology of *Pride & Prejudice*. From these points of departure, Darcy and Elizabeth take fanciful (and sometimes fantastical) alternate paths to their happy ending.

These Regency shorts presuppose fluency with the characters and plot of *Pride & Prejudice*. For any readers unacquainted with the original, I strongly recommend first reading Jane Austen's classic novel (free e-book and in print at local libraries) or, at the very least, viewing one of several movie adaptations. Doing so will greatly enhance understanding and enjoyment of this collection.

*A word about short stories...*

In Vienna, not far from the Stephansdom with its spectacular chevron roof, resides an apartment once denominated Figarohaus. I wandered through the rooms and imagined life for Mozart's family, but these many years later, what I recall best was my initial exposure to a chamber concert. A few talented musicians produced the most delightful music. I was enchanted.

If a novel is composed for a symphony orchestra, then short stories must be arranged for a chamber ensemble—neither so long nor so complex, but no less beautiful or moving. And with that, dear reader, I invite you to liberate your imagination and lose yourself in the whimsy and intimacy of a little chamber music—or as it is sometimes described, a conversation among friends.

Renée Beyea
Del Rio, Texas

# CONCEPTION

She whirled past so quick it seemed
A flash of light, a whispered dream—
A rush of skirts, of skipping feet,
Of dark, bright eyes and laughter sweet.

Yet from my hand she twirled away,
And how I laughed to see her play!
What joy, what goodness she would bring;
I could not wait to hear her sing.

Pursued until her cheeks grew pink,
I captured her in ageless ink,
And from the page she smiled at me
With one brow arched so charmingly.

Then came in twos and threes and tens,
The relatives, militia, friends,

To sing her song all were agreed.
Just one more person did I need—

I felt his eyes where day meets night,
By shadows hid at edge of sight.
Oh, how I coaxed, cajoled and teased,
But he was firm, would not be pleased—

At least until he heard her voice;
Her sparkling wit gainsaid his choice.
Then out he came, his posture straight,
With noble brow and regal gait.

So tall, so handsome and so proud,
He strode to her and stately bowed.
She curtseyed but his hand refused.
I watched, enraptured and amused.

Too late he found I'd bound his will
And held him fast beneath my quill.
He frowned, he glared; I saw my chance,
Arranged my lines to lead their dance.

And dancing still, they're fixed in time,
Their lives reformed, their hearts entwined.
Thus might have sprung from fertile thought
The story that Jane Austen wrought.

# WORDS IN THE WIND

"Steady to his purpose, he scarcely spoke ten words to her through the whole of Saturday, and though they were at one time left by themselves for half an hour, he adhered most conscientiously to his book, and would not even look at her."

*Pride & Prejudice*, Volume I, Chapter 12

"Lizzy," the hushed voice urged, "Lizzy, please wake."

Rousing herself was like climbing a steep hill. Elizabeth rolled toward her bed companion. "What is it?"

"Someone is in our room." Jane's voice trembled.

"You have only been dreaming again." Elizabeth found her sister's shaking hand where she gripped the cover's edge. "Go back to sleep."

"No, I am certain this time. Over there," Jane's fingers were barely discernible pointing toward the door, "I saw a cloaked figure and heard the swish of fabric."

Elizabeth sighed. Trying to reason with her sister in this state would only upset her further. Instead, she sat up, swung her feet to the floor, and fumbled for the low-burning taper to light her bedside candle. Ominous shadows towered against the walls.

"See?" She turned back to Jane. "No one."

Jane was peering about, the bedclothes held tight beneath her chin, her eyes wide and troubled.

Elizabeth smiled and shook her head as she crossed to the door. "You only mistook my cloak for an intruder." She extended the limp folds. "Nothing is lurking within it, save my reticule, I assure you."

"I am sorry to disturb you." Jane exhaled a long breath. "Forgive me?"

"Of course." Elizabeth gazed at her, pricked with guilt that her sweet sister should be haunted by frightening dreams. She returned to the bed, extinguished the candle and slipped under the quilt, grateful to escape the autumn chill.

"I should be the one asking you to forgive me," Elizabeth said.

"Whatever for?"

"For reading Radcliffe to you before we retired."

"But her stories bring you such amusement."

"Only you would forfeit your rest for my amusement."

"Your laughter makes me happy."

"And your peaceful slumber makes me happy."

"I will make every effort not to wake you in the future," Jane said.

"No, no, you must not think you are to blame." Elizabeth squeezed her sister's hand. "I only meant no more gothic novels at night."

A tree limb's tip rapped like fingers on the glass.

"Her novels are horrid, you know," Jane said.

"As they are intended to be." Elizabeth laughed lightly. "Please do not be ashamed of your sensibilities. It is only because you are goodness itself and have the tenderest heart."

They bade each other pleasant dreams, and Jane began to recite a familiar, comforting psalm under her breath.

Elizabeth listened until sleep silenced her sister, and then the night sounds stirred her imagination. Branches scraped the window panes like ghoulish claws seeking entry. The wind keened at the casements and hurled itself against the walls. She laughed to herself. Who needed Radcliffe anyway?

Heavy clouds still obstructed the moon, but at least the interminable rain had ceased and the wind would make for a drier walk come morning.

*****

The sun had not yet risen when Elizabeth woke. Good. She did not oversleep. She eased from the mattress, not wanting to wake her sister, and went about her morning preparations with practiced efficiency. She pulled on long woolen stockings, her warmest day dress, and over that a thick pelisse. She made a hasty toilette, patting her face with cold water and pinning her hair by touch alone. Darkness shrouded her reflection, but she dared not light a candle. Not that it mattered, since she was unlikely to meet anyone on her errand.

At the door, she settled the cloak that troubled Jane in the night about her shoulders, fastened the frog clasps across her bosom, and slid her reticule onto her elbow. Her walking boots she hoisted in one hand. Better to transit the house in the stealth of stocking feet. Neither sisters nor servants would raise an eyebrow at her pre-dawn departure, but she did want to avoid Mr. Collins. He might find it necessary to chaperone her into Meryton.

She eased the door open and then closed it behind her, willing the hinges not to squeak. She stood in the darkened hall, waiting for her eyes to adjust. Several doors rattled and rasped, and the ceiling grumbled overhead. Longbourn House creaked and moaned like an arthritic grandmother, but it was only the servants moving about and the wind probing for entrance. She crept down the right side of the staircase, hugging the wall and avoiding the steps that groaned.

On the ground floor, Elizabeth lit a candle and descended yet further. The stillroom door yawned, a black maw waiting to devour her—until her light cast the swags of drying vegetation in relief. Their shadows might have been a cave bristling with stalactites or talons in a dragon's lair. She giggled. With quick, deft movements, she began to form two posies from the dried flowers racked above her. She reached for a spray of lavender, inhaling its clean, pungent aroma, and a white scrap of paper drifted to the work table. She snatched it and read,

III. How I should like to plumb the depths of your mind and mine the treasures of your soul.

How very odd. Who had written it and for whom? And why the numeral three? But she did not have time to puzzle it out and slipped it into her reticule. The posies finished, she bound them in a cloth to shield them from the wind.

One more stop to make.

In the kitchen, Cook shook her head as she placed a cup of tea and a hot roll before Elizabeth.

"I hope you wrapped up good, Miss Lizzy. 'Tis bitter out this morning."

"Thank you, Cook," she said around a savory mouthful. She swallowed. "I shall be warmed from the inside out."

"Go on with you now." Cook turned back to her baking, but Elizabeth did not miss the smile that creased her face.

At the front door, Elizabeth stepped into one boot and then the other. A crinkling sound made her wrench her toes back. She overturned her boot and shook it, but nothing fell out. She reached in gingerly and withdrew another small piece of paper. This one said,

II. You are beauty and elegance, wit and mirth, goodness and compassion united.

Elizabeth resisted rolling her eyes and stuffed the paper into her reticule with the first. Someone was playing games with her. Lydia would be the most likely to think it a fine joke, but she would never have spared the effort. Perhaps she had put Kitty up to it. They might have copied the sentences from the novel over which they had been tittering. With the rain confining them to the house and their spirits high in eagerness for Netherfield's ball, it was no wonder if they forged their own entertainment.

She tied her boots, straightened, and secured her bonnet before pulling up the hood of her cloak. She donned one tight glove and was wrestling with the other, except the third finger would not cooperate. She pulled and pushed, and in exasperation turned it nearly inside out, only to find a tightly rolled cylinder of paper gleaming from where her finger ought to have been. This was really too much, but she unrolled it all the same.

IV. In you, there is nothing wanting.

Elizabeth smirked. That could not be true of anyone—except possibly Jane. She supposed Kitty and Lydia meant to tease her about her partiality for Wickham, but what if another had stumbled on the papers among her things? That might have necessitated a difficult explanation. Her sisters were taking it a bit far. Yet again, she would have to speak with them about the impropriety of their behavior, not that it would have much effect.

Finally, she was out the door and traversing the gravel drive. The wind grabbed her cloak and blew it behind her. She wrestled it back into compliance and clutched both sides tight. Cook was correct. Not only was the day bitter, it was blustery. She examined the low, grey sky. The clouds looked pregnant, but the ground was fairly dry. An umbrella would be useless in the wind. Surely she could make it to Meryton and back before the rain resumed. Her errand there would only take a few minutes. She need not linger.

Thus decided, she hurried down the drive and turned onto the road, treading the firmer edge and staying out of the muddy ruts. The wind whistled in the branches and rattled the drying leaves. She had the uneasy sensation of being watched. Twice she turned to see if she were being followed, but without the sun to illumine the distance, the empty road only disappeared into the gloom.

When a cart coming from town approached, Elizabeth stepped aside to wait near the entrance to Whitley Farm and avoid a splattering from the wheels. She exchanged a friendly wave with the driver and moved to resume her course, but a bizarre sight arrested her. A paper strip flapped where it was suspended high in the hedge. She set the posies aside and stood on tiptoe to retrieve it. Indeed, it was just the size of the others she had found, except this one was caught in a spider's web. That eliminated her sisters as suspects. Though the moisture had caused the ink to run somewhat, she was able to read,

V. I would love you as you are worthy of being loved, with all the faithfulness and generosity, nobility and sacrifice of which man is capable.

This was a noble sentiment indeed and, joined with the three which had preceded it, incited her heart to a momentary flutter. Who could the author be? The only man of her acquaintance whom she could envision making such a declaration was Wickham. Perhaps he had connived with her sisters to secret the other papers at Longbourn. But a spider's web did not seem a prudent hiding place at all. If she had not stopped for the cart at that precise location, she would have missed it.

Elizabeth perused the paper again before tucking it in her reticule and reclaiming her packet of posies. She could not approve the method, of course, but she was flattered. The words were a trifle studied and lacked his easy charm, yet what woman would not wish to be loved in such a way?

Thoughts whirling, she gazed past Whitley's barn. Movement in the periphery of her vision drew her attention to the barn door as it opened and a figure emerged. He was not ten yards distant, and even in the low light, she recognized him at once. He must have been attempting to conceal himself after securing the paper to the web. For a moment, Elizabeth thought to pass by before he saw her, but then their eyes met and she waved.

"Good morning, Mr. Wickham," she called.

"Why, Miss Bennet!" He hastened toward her and exchanged a bow for her curtsey. "How unexpected to see you about so early on this fine morning."

"Fine is doubtful," she said, glancing at the leaden skies with a smile, "but surely you cannot mean my presence is wholly unexpected." How else would he have known where to hide the paper, if her sisters had not informed him of her route?

He looked bemused and glanced back at the barn. "Unexpected does not necessarily imply unwelcome."

"I should hope not." The teasing lilt in her voice recalled his attention, and she blushed under his gaze.

His eyes drifted again. He cleared his throat. "If you are on your way to Meryton, may I offer escort?"

"Thank you," she said but did not accept his arm. She could hardly broach a topic suspended between them as delicately as that gossamer web, yet she must make some acknowledgement.

"Miss Bennet," he prompted with some impatience, "let us away."

Once they commenced strolling side by side, she said, "I have stumbled on quite the mystery this morning."

"Have you?" His look of alarm was swiftly surmounted by a smile. "I should like to know more."

"First, I was hoping you might hint as to the location of numeral one as well as to how many I am to expect."

"I am afraid I have not the pleasure of understanding you."

She paused and turned to gauge his expression, but either he was superb in his disguise or he was honestly ignorant. But if Wickham had not authored the papers—

Over his shoulder, she saw the door to the other end of Whitley's barn swing wide and produce a young woman. Elizabeth observed her movements, and a sickening suspicion dawned.

Wickham turned to follow her gaze.

The woman's hands had finished arranging the bodice of her dress and were piling raven locks atop her head as she moved away toward the farmhouse. Elizabeth watched between her and Wickham. His face turned ashen, more so than she could credit the dim, colorless morning.

"You need not look at me like that." He drew himself up and made a derisive sound at the back of his throat. "I have already told you that I am no Darcy."

"Pardon?"

"To be as virtuous as a maiden?" He scoffed. "It is unnatural, I tell you."

He spoke as if she should likewise discredit Darcy for such principles, but she could only gape at his indelicacy and wish the conversation at an end.

"But come, Miss Bennet, I see that I have made you uncomfortable." He was all charm again and possessed himself of her fingers before she could react.

"Please unhand me, Mr. Wickham."

He did not and a frisson of fear snaked through her. He made an elaborate bow over her glove and bent as if to kiss her hand.

"I fear, madam," he said as he straightened and released her, "that this small delay has obliged me to return to my quarters with all haste. I regret I shall not be able to accompany you after all and pray you will overlook the slight."

"Please," she said with relief, though with no intention of overlooking his behavior, "do not let me detain you a moment longer."

Their parting exchange was civil, and it was not long before the shadows swallowed him.

So Wickham was a libertine. Elizabeth lowered her head against the wind, one hand clutching her cloak and the other her flowers, and plowed forward. How foolish she was to have been captivated by his charms—foolish, disappointed, and disgusted. How could she have misread him?

She replayed their conversations in her memory. Most prominent were his insinuations about Darcy, information which in retrospect was unseemly for him to divulge, especially on so brief an acquaintance. Why had she not seen it before? Could she trust the accuracy of Wickham's account? She swallowed back a sick feeling in her stomach. She had encouraged Wickham and endorsed his contempt.

Of Darcy it was now imperative, if not to think well, at least to allow him some opportunity to defend himself. Nor was Wickham's denunciation lost on her. Pride and incivility aside, Darcy had risen in her estimation as abruptly as Wickham had fallen. Whatever his failings, Darcy remained a gentleman.

Elizabeth paused near an intersection and looked about. Where was she? In her distraction, she had nearly missed the side street which was the shortest route to the church.

She turned and had not walked more than ten steps when she spied something small and pale in the middle of the road. Her preoccupation had forced the mysterious papers from her mind. With a glance around to confirm no one was coming and she was unobserved, she moved into the lane and crouched to retrieve another scrap of paper. She employed her bottom hem to wipe away the grime until she could discern the letters.

VI. I can see you now, cheeks aglow and eyes sparkling, and only your maid to remark on your gown's dirty hem.

She stood quickly, one hand against the sudden warmth in her cheek, and scanned the street lined with shops. Light flickered in several apartment windows above stairs, the proprietors not yet descended to their labors, but she did not detect any observers. How could the writer have depicted her at this very moment and with such precision? This reintroduced the question of identity, for she was now convinced the author was neither her sister nor Wickham. Who was he, and how did he come to place these notes in her path? She folded the paper in half and added it to her collection.

Another minute's walk brought her to the churchyard's side gate. She stopped to peer over the stone wall. The long half-light that preceded dawn had yielded to a bleak sunrise nearly obscured by the threatening clouds. The wind moaned in the trees and buffeted the tombstones standing in crooked rows like aged soldiers, yet it did not disturb the peace.

Elizabeth grasped the low iron gate and began to swing it inwards. A rock centered like a finial atop a gate pillar fixed her notice. The baffling appearances were beginning to unnerve her, yet she could not resist their allure. She rested her package on the pillar and tugged the paper from under the stone. It read,

VII. I long for you, companion of my heart and mind.

A twig snapped somewhere above her head, and she jumped. She forced a laugh. The mystifying papers had spooked her more effectively than a Radcliffe novel. How very silly! She had yet to uncover a rational explanation, but one certainly existed. She read the sentence once more, and her fear dissolved with the words. A smile tugged at her lips. She longed for a companion of heart and mind as well. She secured the paper in her reticule and the posies in her arm, and then she picked her way to a corner of the graveyard shadowed by an enormous oak.

Her eyes scanned the perimeter fence. But for the wind assaulting the leaves overhead, all was tranquil and empty. Satisfied she was alone, she focused on her purpose. She ambled along, her hand resting on a cross here and a coping there as she named all the Bennets and Gardiners and the generations who had preceded them.

Elizabeth paused before a tiny marker and read again the words that stunned her when she first discovered them: *William Bennet, b. 10 October 1788 - d. 10 August 1789. Beloved son.* Ten months. For ten months there had been a Bennet heir, a son to break the estate's entail and secure the family name. How altered her mother might have been had her brother lived. But he was never mentioned. She unwrapped the dried flowers and placed the smaller bouquet on her brother's grave. He died before Jane was born, but the memorial spoke to her of life's unpredictable and ephemeral nature.

Four more headstones remained before her final stop, and she had nearly passed them when her eye snagged on the now familiar flash of white. She leaned down and retrieved the paper tucked neatly at the footing of her great-grandmother's gravestone. She stood and angled it for the best light.

VIII. You challenge and inspire and delight me.

She darted another look around the walled yard, then cocked an eyebrow. She refused to be unsettled. Whoever he was, she appreciated the direction of his thoughts. She grinned and addressed her dead ancestors as if they could hear. "What do you think? Shall I excuse the gentleman his bold disregard for propriety?"

Two more steps and she knelt beside her grandfather's grave to gently deposit the remaining posy. Elizabeth rested a hand on the stone and gazed with fondness at his name.

"I miss you, Grandfather. I wish you were here." He had been a favorite with her just as she was his favorite. From him she learned to appreciate the out of doors, from him she inherited her love of rambling over the countryside. Her father could sit all day in his book room, but his father had to be out in the fresh air. She inhaled a deep breath, and the cold made her cough.

She laughed and patted the stone before rising. "You would appreciate today. Even the weather could not stop me from coming."

She turned and found her grandfather standing before her, wrapped in a dark cloak and a deep-brimmed hat, his withered shoulders restored to their once broad proportions. She squeezed her lids closed and opened them again. The apparition began to approach. She cried out, stepped back, and then danced sideways in an attempt to avoid treading on the grave.

"Miss Bennet." The voice was gravelly. Long fingers sheathed in a menacing glove stretched toward her. But he did not halt.

Elizabeth was frantic for a means of escape, but her grandfather's headstone hemmed her in the corner of the yard. The stone wall was too high for her to vault. "Sir, I beg you," she said, her voice trembling, "please come no farther."

The figure stopped ten feet away in a towering swirl of black, like midnight embodied. "Miss Bennet, you need not fear. It is I," and so saying, he removed the hat that made it difficult to recognize his face, "Fitzwilliam Darcy."

Her heart raced as she stared at him. To have mistaken Mr. Darcy for a graveyard specter? She almost laughed in her hysteria and relief.

He was studying her in apparent concern, his brows drawn together. He was the last person she would ever have expected to meet. What sinister purpose did he have in the Meryton graveyard—and at this hour? She shuddered.

"You are cold," he observed.

"My cloak is warm enough," she said and pulled it tighter about her.

"Why are you here?"

She thought she should be the one asking. "To give thanks for my forebears and visit their final resting place."

"I see." He nodded, but his brow remained creased.

"Longbourn does not boast its own cemetery. I come each year on the anniversary of my grandfather's death. He was very dear to me, and—" Why was she babbling? She commanded herself to be quiet.

"You come alone?"

Perhaps she should have brought a maid for propriety's sake, though she would rather not sacrifice the solitude. "Jane would accompany me if I asked, but my younger sisters think it macabre."

"I think it shows an admirable degree of honor and respect."

Elizabeth raised both brows. Was he complimenting her? They stood blinking at each other for several awkward moments.

"Mr. Darcy, now you have learned my reason, I confess an equal degree of curiosity as to why you are here. Surely you do not have family likewise at rest in Hertfordshire."

"I do not."

She smiled. "Is that all the answer I am to expect?"

He shifted his feet and frowned.

"If you will excuse me," she said, lifting her chin and weary of awaiting his answer—for clearly he was not going to oblige her in sketching his character—"I have concluded my visit and must be returning home before I am missed."

"Of course." His bow was all politeness. "I wish you a good day, Miss Bennet."

"And a good day to you, Mr. Darcy." She curtseyed and made to hurry past him.

The next instant, her toes bloomed with pain and she hurtled toward him, arms flailing for balance. Alarm overspread his face, then dark wool filled her vision and her nose collided with his chest. He smelled of leather, horses, and an inviting pungency akin to the aroma of tea leaves.

His hands steadied her shoulders as he assisted her to regain her footing. How humiliating. Elizabeth glanced behind her before stepping away. The guilty corner of the grave curb glared back with glee. The wind too seemed to be dancing in delight as it tore at her hood and tried to bury them in a flurry of leaves. A flicker of white passed before her face, and she seized it.

"Are you well?" he asked.

She nodded but could only stare at the identical paper he now gripped between his fingers. She looked down at her own. This one was unnumbered and read,

He went there to register.

She turned it over, only to find the expected numeral on the reverse.

IX. It is stronger than death, stronger than the grave.

"This cannot be correct," she murmured. The sentence bore no continuity to the others, like a puzzle piece from the wrong puzzle.

Darcy wore a severe frown as he examined his own paper. He raised his eyes and caught her gaze. "What does yours say?"

She froze in debate. That he would even ask was inappropriate. They were private words. But he did not appear any more surprised than she to snatch words from the wind, and the circumstance was beyond astonishment. Her curiosity won over discretion. She extended the paper to him. He handed his to her in exchange.

She read again,

IX. Nothing can quench the love I have for you.

"I think this one belongs to me," she said, unaccountable relief flooding through her at the declaration from her unknown admirer.

"It does, does it?" His frown transformed to a smile.

She could not help but note how well it became him, not that she could see anything humorous. "They must have been switched."

"Tell me, Miss Bennet, have you any other papers like these?"

She hesitated. "Yes. Why do you ask?"

"May I have them?" He might have shifted a trifle closer.

She stepped back. "Why should I give them to you? What is your interest in them?"

"These— these notes were published without the author's permission. I seek to recover them."

"You know the identity of the author then?" Her heart quickened at the possibility.

"I do."

"And how they came to be hidden in my boots and gloves and along my path this morning?"

He started and his complexion grew ruddier. "No. I am not privy to that knowledge."

"Then I have a proposal," she said, merriment creeping into her tone as she peered up at him from under her lashes. Had he always been so very tall? His discomfort almost made him charming. "I will relinquish the papers to you on condition that you relinquish his name to me."

"That is hardly fair."

"You wish to recover the papers, and I wish to discover the author. It seems a fair exchange."

He considered her so intently that Elizabeth began to chafe under his direct gaze. She reached to tuck a stray lock behind her ear. Perhaps she should have given more time to her toilette after all. An indecipherable expression passed over his face as fleeting as a cloud across the sun.

"I answered why you should give the papers to me," he said. "Now, may I ask why I should disclose their author? What is your interest in him?"

Heat suffused her face as she recalled the sequence of intimate confessions, made all the worse by her embarrassment that she should blush before him. "That is private information, sir."

"And what you request is not?"

She mirrored his arched brow.

"If you would indulge me"—he sighed—"I need to understand your reasoning." At least he was making an amended effort to be polite and express sincere interest.

How imperative was it that she learn the author's identity? Was it merely idle curiosity or something more? But she would always wonder and regret not making the attempt. Her boot toed the late autumn grass. She was too mortified to look at him.

"Is it any surprise that a lady should be gratified and desire to know the name of her admirer"—the words fell from her lips quiet and soft, and she sensed him leaning nearer—"that...that she might determine whether or not she wishes to return the sentiments?"

When she raised her eyes to his, he looked away swiftly and said nothing. Was he going to renege on their agreement?

"Come, Mr. Darcy," she coaxed after a minute of quiet, "I have been forthright with you."

At length, he returned his attention to her. "I know neither who copied out the sentences on the fragments of foolscap nor how they came to be in your possession, but the words themselves—"

Her heart pattered in anticipation.

He held her gaze and took a deep breath. "The words are mine. I composed them in my journal."

Elizabeth tried not to gape. Mr. Darcy kept a journal? He was the author? "But you do not like me," she spluttered. "You only look at me to find fault."

"No." His head rotated slowly from side to side. "If that is what you believe, then I was overly successful in concealing my admiration."

But her mind was too occupied with the revelation to ponder his response. His words comprised every sentence that had strummed her heart like the strings of a harp. He had written of love and longing. About her. She regarded him, marveling, and her perspective shifted. Who was this man, tall and handsome, proud and principled, who contemplated her with unnerving intensity, who professed his admiration so ardently? She had judged him arrogant and undeserving, when she did not know him at all. But she wished to. Such a conclusion surprised her, and she laughed.

His intensity melted into a smile—a gentle, earnest smile that she had provoked. "May I inquire what amuses you?"

"Only how rapidly my opinion can be overturned," she waved a hand, "that and the whole improbable circumstance. But, Mr. Darcy, if you did not hide the papers, then who did?"

"I have had many hours to contemplate that difficulty, and every conjecture has proved unsupportable. You mentioned finding one of the papers in your glove?"

She confirmed this and proceeded to detail the location of each. "It must be someone who has access to my room and my belongings." She shivered. Perhaps Jane had not been dreaming after all.

"If only the answer were so simple."

"What do you mean?"

"I too followed a trail of papers, each with a clue as to the location of the next. They are what led me here."

"So either this individual has access to both residences and our personal effects, or at least two people have been united in their endeavors." She shook her head in consternation. "But to take such great care and effort—and to what end? It is very puzzling."

"Is it?" Darcy asked in a low voice. "I have reached the conclusion that this"—he gestured between them—

"is the end, the goal, that the papers were intended to draw us here."

"To the graveyard?"

"To one another. It is"—he swallowed—"providential and I should not like to question Providence too narrowly."

She would have teased him for his lack of curiosity were not his aspect quite so solemn. She was not satisfied on that account, but there would be time enough to investigate later.

"There is one matter on which I would like to reassure myself," he added.

"Yes?"

"That no papers remain outstanding. I should not wish for any to fall into the wrong hands." He opened one gloved palm. "If you would lend me the notes?"

"Of course." What Miss Bingley might do with such knowledge made Elizabeth tremble. She turned aside to rest her reticule atop the enclosure and delve into it. She handed the slips to him one by one, and he produced a matching handful from his coat pocket. He began arranging them side by side until there were two neat rows, one of eight and one of nine, staring back at her from the stone wall. When had the morning grown so very calm? The wind did not so much as whisper.

"Do you have another?" he said. "There ought to be nine."

"I only found eight," she said but scoured her reticule anyway. There it was—pinned with care to the lining.

Her own name flashed before her as she handed the paper to him.

He set it in place. "You may read it, if you wish. You already know the half. It is right that you know the whole."

She cast an anxious glance at the sky but could only perceive a uniform slate beyond the sheltering trees. The anemic sun appeared to have ceded the fight, for its faded light had dimmed yet further. She leaned over to better see the words, but even as she began to read, she was acutely conscious of Darcy's presence beside her, of the rise and fall of his chest, of the manner in which his fist clenched and unclenched at his side.

I. My dearest Elizabeth, for such I would wish to call you.
I. You fill my days and haunt my dreams; I have never been so bewitched by a woman.

II. You are beauty and elegance, wit and mirth, goodness and compassion united.
II. You are everything I have desired in a wife.

III. How I should like to plumb the depths of your mind and mine the treasures of your soul.
III. What riches await the man who truly knows you!

IV. In you, there is nothing wanting.

IV. Were I your husband, I would devote myself to your happiness.

V. I would love you as you are worthy of being loved, with all the faithfulness and generosity, nobility and sacrifice of which man is capable.
V. If only I could whisk you away and settle you as mistress of Pemberley—how you would delight in its walks and woods!

VI. I can see you now, cheeks aglow and eyes sparkling, and only your maid to remark on your gown's dirty hem.
VI. Such a sister you would be to my own—you are precisely what she needs—precisely what I need.

VII. I long for you, companion of my heart and mind.
VII. You are my perfect match.

VIII. You challenge and inspire and delight me.
VIII. Would that I might do the same for you.

IX. Nothing can quench the love I have for you.
IX. It is stronger than death, stronger than the grave.

When Elizabeth finished, she did not know if she could meet his gaze. The frosty air was a balm to her burning cheeks. How was she to respond to such a confession? What must he be thinking? She spared a glance at him.

Darcy was watching her with such an expression of tenderness and hope.

"I am honored, sir, to have inspired this degree of admiration and" —she choked a little—"and love."

"You must believe me—I do not expect, that is…" His tentative smile wavered further. "I see that this has taken you by surprise, and I am not so unreasonable as to expect you to return my sentiments at present. But the secrets of my heart are laid bare before you. If you might—if you might give me any reason to hope—I—"

Before she knew what she was doing, she pressed his forearm with her hand. "It is safe to hope, Mr. Darcy."

She looked up into his face at his broad, intelligent brow, at how expressive his mouth was if she paused to attend, but something caught her in the eye. She blinked twice in succession. Cold fingers tapped her nose, her forehead, her cheek. A chorus of patters began in the tree above, joined the next moment by a bass rhythm against the gravestones.

"Quickly, Miss Bennet," Darcy swept the papers into one hand while the other at her elbow propelled her forward, "to the church."

They raced through the increasing rain and gained the door just as it became a downpour. Darcy shoved it open with his shoulder and pulled her in behind him. They stood for a moment, breathing hard and peering out into the murky waterfall. The rain spattered from the stone steps into the narthex, wetting the hem of her cloak and the toes of his boots. It thundered against the slate roof.

Darcy reached over her shoulder to close the door, and the movement placed her within the circle of his arms. Dark enveloped them. She could barely make out his profile silhouetted against the wan light filtering in from the sanctuary. He did not withdraw, and her heart commenced a jig. His hands traveled across her shoulders, and his fingers settled beneath her chin. She should move or speak, but she could not think for the peculiar thrumming in her ears. His breath was moist against her cheek, as if in warning, and then his lips found hers. She gasped in shock, but there was no air, only an infinite tenderness that chased every chill from her veins.

When he released her, she staggered back. One hand groped behind her for the wall. Glory.

"I am sorry, Elizabeth. I—" His contrite voice was near. "Did I frighten you?"

"No." What she felt was nothing akin to fear. "No, but if you might allow me a moment—"

His boots scuffed the paving stones as he moved away. She dug her fingers into the rough wall and placed the back of her other hand against her tingling lips. Laughter burbled in her throat. Mr. Darcy had kissed her. And in the church, no less. This was supposed to come at the end of courtship, not the beginning.

Light flared, bathing the narthex in a golden hue. Darcy stood several feet away, before a table holding a candle and the parish register. The ninth clue, of course. Elizabeth moved to join him, though she could not imagine what more this might reveal after what had already been disclosed.

He turned the pages methodically, but she saw it first, there in the binding, a blank foolscap marker. She reversed it and laid it across the page that they might read together.

X. I offer you all that I am and all that I have, if only you will grant me the honor of your hand.

He had written to propose marriage? Her thoughts swirled, and she felt like she had lost her footing in a shallow pool and was sinking under the waters.

"Miss Bennet, do not be distressed." Darcy's deep voice recalled her. He lifted the small paper and rested it in his palm. "I neither regret nor retract these words, but"—his dark eyes mirrored the candlelight when he turned them on her—"let it be enough that my intention is clear, and when you are ready, I will renew the offer. Is that agreeable to you?"

She nodded in relief. "Thank you for your consideration, sir. Are there—are there any more papers to find?"

He smiled and shook his head. "There cannot be more, for that was the concluding sentence to my—to what I had written of you."

The mysterious words may have come to an end, but much remained to be said. She hardly knew where to begin. She passed her hand over the register and grasped the leather cover, happy for a moment's delay. Pages fluttered and settled as she closed the volume, skimming past all the births and deaths, baptisms and marriages.

Familiar handwriting caught her eye and she stopped, her pulse accelerating. The same careful script that distinguished each scrap of paper stared up from among the other entries in the parish record.

Darcy scooted the candle closer. It read,

X. Married 2 March 1812 Fitzwilliam Darcy, master of Pemberley and Elizabeth Bennet, spinster of this parish

There was a sharp intake of breath beside her ear, and Darcy rested a hand heavily on the table. "But who wrote this?"

"Who indeed?" She repeated in wonderment and reached to run her finger over their joined names and the date—in ten tens of days if she calculated correctly. Their union seemed preordained, as if somehow the ribbon of their lives had folded and bypassed all the intervening months. She thought she ought to feel something other than what she did—irritation or apprehension or even anticipation—but it was as if the serenity of that holy place had soothed away her earlier anxiety and she knew only certainty.

The words shifted without warning. Elizabeth slid the foolscap strip from the book.

Darcy was quiet and she could not look at him, but she touched her gloved fingers to his.

"Mr. Darcy," she said, passing the final X to him, "when you renew your offer, I think this shall be a fitting answer."

# EPILOGUE

(for any in doubt of what followed)

If Elizabeth's younger sisters teased her about her more than usually careful preparations in advance of Bingley's ball, she only smiled, smoothed her hands down the rich fabric of her best gown, and let them think what they may. And if, after greeting the Netherfield hosts, Elizabeth's gaze combed every public room before she was informed Wickham was unable to attend, she only commented with private relief that it was no great loss.

But when her eyes landed on the object of her search, she smiled. For Mr. Darcy's eyes were on her, had been for some time she surmised. He smiled, such a look of warmth and tenderness diffusing over his face as warmed her in return. He came to her across the breadth of the ballroom as if he were drawn by some invisible tether that had irrevocably bound them that cold morning in the graveyard.

"Mr. Darcy," she said and curtseyed deeply.

"Miss Bennet," he replied with an equally deferential bow. "I hope you have reserved a set or two for me."

"A set perhaps, if you will ask," she quirked a brow, "but two? How my mother would talk."

"Let her." He smiled again. "If you are not engaged, may I have the honor of the first?"

She squirmed. "I am afraid that in my excitement for the ball I was obliged to my cousin, lest I be forced to sit out the entire evening."

He nodded in empathy. "The second, then?"

"Mr. Bingley has preceded you there."

He frowned. "Are you engaged for the supper set?"

"It shall be the pinnacle of my evening to accompany you."

"And lest I find myself supplanted again, may I also request the last?"

"With pleasure," she said and, recalling what happened in the church, added, "though I begin to think precipitance is your habit."

He laughed and she laughed with him, the joy of the evening welling within her and suffusing her countenance with a rosy brilliance. Any fears she entertained that Darcy might have rethought his confession or that she might regret her equally rash acquiescence were banished in their first exchange.

If Sir William Lucas interrupted their dancing to remark on their elegance and lightness of foot and to comment on Mr. Bingley's apparent preference for Miss Bennet, Darcy only glanced at his friend and her sister in beneficence.

"You seem pleased, sir," said Elizabeth as they resumed their places in line.

"I am," he said. "For once my friend has preceded me in discerning from the first how enchanting and agreeable are the eldest Misses Bennet."

It would have been extraordinary indeed if Mr. Darcy's particular attentions to Miss Elizabeth Bennet went unremarked, but they did not. The neighborhood found it easy to forgive the pride and incivility of so great a man once he saw fit to bestow his affections on one of their own. It was counted odd, however, when Mr. Bingley removed to town for a brief stay that his sisters should follow and leave poor Mr. Darcy without a host at Netherfield. He seemed to make the best of it, though, and was known to frequent Longbourn for dinner and stay through supper. If he was seen in the Hertfordshire lanes with Miss Elizabeth on his arm and Miss Bennet and Miss Mary trailing a discreet distance behind, it warranted a wink and a knowing nod.

If Wickham's residence in Meryton was curtailed prematurely and his commission resigned, only the youngest and silliest maidens mourned his departure. No one was disposed to question either the motives or information of the estimable Mr. Darcy or those of Mr. Bennet, who roused himself enough to second his soon-to-be son in exposing the scoundrel.

If Elizabeth frowned a little when Darcy shared with her the full entry in his journal, it was not to be wondered at, for she did feel the slight. There was a difficult conversation to be had and explanations and apologies to be made on both sides, but each was eager to please. Being persuaded that her intended was sincere in the amendment of his attitude, if not yet wholly improved in practice, Elizabeth forgave. They agreed that a lesson learned early was less painful than one learned late.

When Mr. Bingley returned to his estate, he adopted his friend's daily pattern of walking out with the Longbourn ladies and dining at their table. Miss Mary was not sorry to cede her position as Miss Bennet's companion. The two couples knew nothing of the long, cold winter through which they passed their courtship, for they had among them love and affection enough to warm the frostiest day.

It was no surprise, therefore, when the engagements were announced, nor when Miss Bennet and Miss Elizabeth exchanged their names for those of Mrs. Bingley and Mrs. Darcy one windy morning in March.

Some years later at Pemberley—ten years to be precise—as she always did on the anniversary of her grandfather's death, Mrs. Darcy opened the small wooden casket designed for this purpose and withdrew the twenty foolscap slips. The paper was beginning to yellow and the ink to fade. She spread them out side by side, ten by ten, and read through the cryptic sentences.

How remarkable that so few words could be the means of commencing the companionship and subsequent marriage both had come to value above any earthly possession or friendship. They never solved the mystery of the copyist, but it mattered not. They had each other.

Fitzwilliam's longer arm and broader hand reached around Elizabeth to finger the cherished objects. His breath tickled her neck when he spoke, and warmth flooded her.

"I am grateful Providence saw fit to expose my secret," he said. "The Lord only knows how long it would have taken me to come to my senses and make a proper proposal."

She turned within his arms and looked up into his face. "Why did you kiss me that day in the church? It was very improper and, now that I know you so well, very uncharacteristic too."

"It was not a matter of thought." His shoulders rose and fell a fraction. "I can hardly account for a moment's impulse."

"That will never do, not from my husband who considers everything with such care and has not an impetuous bone in his body." She laughed and removed a little further to search the dark sincerity of his eyes. "I was still somewhat shocked by the whole affair, and then you took me completely by surprise."

"What can I say? You were there, fresh and lovely and glowing on that grey day, melting in my arms while the rain poured outside, and those words—my words— were still pounding in my heart—" He traced his fingers across her brow and down her cheek and exhaled. "I suppose I was jubilant with the hope of you, and I wanted to claim you, to seal those confessions as truth."

"I cannot condone the moral, but I will admit I am glad." She pulled his coat lapels through her fingers.

"My darling Elizabeth, surely you have realized by now that I cannot resist kissing you." He chuckled softly and made good on his words.

# EXTRACTS *from* Darcy's Journal

*Friday, 15 November 1811, Netherfield*

Elizabeth abides yet at Netherfield though Miss Bennet is on the mend. I both wish for and dread her departure. Dining with her and sitting with her after dinner is the most agreeable agony. She is a pleasure to observe. I admire the unaffected grace of her figure and carriage—and her eyes. I shall not dwell further on their fineness. She is equally a delight to listen to, whether she is baiting me with her wit or rivaling the songbirds with her voice.

She attracts me more than I thought possible, and I fear that I am in some danger. Even now my thoughts are traitors that insist on darting off to compose paeans of love! Perhaps I shall give them words and, in committing them to paper, silence their clamoring:

"My dearest Elizabeth, for such I would wish to call you. You fill my days and haunt my dreams; I have never been so bewitched by a woman. You are beauty and elegance, wit and mirth, goodness and compassion united. You are everything I have desired in a wife. How I should like to plumb the depths of your mind and mine the treasures of your soul. What riches await the man who truly knows you! In you, there is nothing wanting.

Were I your husband, I would devote myself to your happiness. I would love you as you are worthy of being loved, with all the faithfulness and generosity, nobility and sacrifice of which man is capable. If only I could whisk you away and settle you as mistress of Pemberley—how you would delight in its walks and woods! I can see you now, cheeks aglow and eyes sparkling, and only your maid to remark on your gown's dirty hem. Such a sister you would be to my own—you are precisely what she needs—precisely what I need.

I long for you, companion of my heart and mind. You are my perfect match. You challenge and inspire and delight me. Would that I might do the same for you. Nothing can quench the love I have for you. It is stronger than death, stronger than the grave. I offer you all that I am and all that I have, if only you will grant me the honor of your hand."

Did ever a man prove himself such a veritable mooncalf? I astonish myself, I who have teased Bingley these several seasons on his attachments and enthusiasms for the fairer sex. And yet, when I reread these sentiments that came so effortlessly, as if they were words whispered in the wind, I read truth. For if it were possible to take Elizabeth as my wife, I would.

It is my heart of hearts that speaks, but the heart must be governed by reason and I have reasons enough. Her want of connections is nothing next to her mother and sisters' want of propriety. To ally myself and my sister with such a family? To besmirch the name and heritage to which I was born? No, in this I must be unselfish and yield to my duty.

However, I fear that I have already paid her too much attention. If she has perceived my admiration and formed any designs, she must be disillusioned. Let me resolve then on the morrow that, save for what civility requires, I shall neither speak with nor look at her and on no account will I seek her company.

*Saturday, 23 November 1811, Netherfield*

My life has taken an abrupt turn in the course of eight days—nay, in the span of the past ten hours. Of these most extraordinary events and the accompanying alteration in my opinions, a detailed account, while essential, must wait until I have sufficient time to do them justice. Time. The clue on that first, humble slip of paper I found was this: "A time for every purpose." How those words have proved true—not only the billiard room clock in which I discovered the second clue—but my very purpose in coming into Hertfordshire. In light of all that occurred this day, I am persuaded it is to love and marry Miss Elizabeth Bennet.

# A FINE STOUT LOVE
## *or* The Efficacy of Poetry

"And so ended his affection," said Elizabeth impatiently. "There has been many a one, I fancy, overcome in the same way. I wonder who first discovered the efficacy of poetry in driving away love!"

"I have been used to consider poetry as the food of love," said Darcy.

"Of a fine, stout, healthy love it may. Everything nourishes what is strong already, but if it be only a slight, thin sort of inclination, I am convinced that one good sonnet will starve it entirely away."

*Pride & Prejudice*, Volume I, Chapter 9

# ELIZABETH'S ACCOUNT

The floorboards sanded her elbows as Elizabeth scooted from under the bed, careful not to clonk her head on the bedrail. Once clear, she sank back on her knees and dusted the treasured volume of John Donne's poetry. It must have slipped from her hands when she fell asleep last night. She stood to replace it on her bedside table and started.

Across the room, her youngest sister was leaning over her desk. When had she entered? Elizabeth's heart began to pound. If Lydia read the scribblings she left exposed on the blotter—

"Lydia," she ordered, "leave it."

Lydia smirked over her shoulder and sprinted for the door, paper in hand.

"No!" Elizabeth shouted. She dropped Donne on the counterpane, skirted the bed, and stopped under the lintel to check the hall. Lydia's bouncing ringlets were just disappearing down the stairs. Elizabeth hastened after, but her sister navigated the steps and swung around the newel post before Elizabeth descended halfway.

Lydia whirled and waved the paper like a handkerchief. "Looking for this?"

Elizabeth sighed and resumed the chase.

"Lizzy has a beau!" Lydia stretched the last word into two taunting syllables.

Elizabeth tracked her chant through sitting and dining rooms and sped into the hall. Her slippers skated on the polished wood and launched her into the wall opposite. She groaned.

Lydia peeked from a doorway with a faux pout. "Poor little Lizzy is too slow."

Elizabeth stormed the corridor and into the parlor, pulse pattering.

Lydia pranced behind Kitty's seat. "Lizzy has a beau!"

"Stop this instant," Elizabeth cried.

"Girls!" Mrs. Bennet brandished her salts as if in threat. "Lower your voices—"

Kitty giggled.

"—and desist from this hoydenish running."

But Lydia skipped past Mary, riffling her book, and whipped by Jane, knocking her needlework to the floor. Their necks craned to follow Lydia's exit. Elizabeth panted her apologies and rushed in pursuit.

Their mother's strident tones trailed behind. "What will Mr. Collins think?"

Elizabeth could not care what their tedious cousin Collins would think. He was cloistered in Papa's book room anyway, and recovering her composition superseded any other consideration.

Lydia sailed out the front entry, a blur of color and skirts and flying hair, leaving the door agape like a shocked bystander. Elizabeth darted in her wake, sans bonnet, shawl, or gloves. A cool autumn breeze danced past, pausing to kiss her heated cheeks before swirling to pile golden leaves against the shrubbery.

Lydia stopped on the grass within the circular drive and waggled the paper overhead. "Come and get it!"

Elizabeth approached, suspicious of the gleam in her eyes.

Lydia rocked from foot to foot, the offending paper fluttering like a flag atop a ship's mast. The words were only idle imaginings but intended solely for Elizabeth's personal diversion. She *must* conceal them.

Elizabeth stretched, balancing on tiptoe and grunting with effort. Her body pressed against her sister's, but her fingers barely reached Lydia's wrist. She stepped back onto her heels, held out her hand, and leveled her fiercest glare. "Give. Me. The. Paper."

"What? You think I should simply hand it to you for nothing? This is too delicious!" Lydia snickered and reciprocated Elizabeth's glare. "Papa will find them very interesting, I'm sure."

"You would not dare."

"I would."

Elizabeth's heart raced. Lydia never did understand their father. He would not be cross but amused—would probably call Elizabeth silly—and she would be mortified by having to explain to him. "Very well—my pin money for the week."

"For the month."

"That is extortion!"

The younger girl shrugged her shoulders.

Elizabeth folded her arms, held her sister's eyes, and refused even a peek at her hostage verses. She was not a Bennet for nothing. She could outlast Lydia for sheer stubbornness.

A gust assaulted them, and Lydia whooped with glee. Elizabeth swiped away the tendrils slapping her face and saw the paper consigned to the blast just as her sister pirouetted from reach. The little chit. She would race to the house in feigned innocence, and Mamma would grant her immunity. This was how it had transpired ever since she was a tiny dimpled thing hiding in her mother's skirts.

The white square tumbled end over end, floating, sinking, and diving like a gull on a coastal draught. Elizabeth raced down the drive, her eyes affixed to the sheet as if she could leash it with a look, but it soared too swift and too high. If only Mamma had not insisted they wait for Mr. Collins to walk into Meryton, then this trouble might have been avoided!

A massive, black charger paraded into view, her paper careening toward its head. The horse scrambled sideways in a flurry of dust and hooves. The rider sprang from the saddle. He seized her paper with one hand and the reins with the other. Her heart froze. Mr. Darcy.

Elizabeth would have fled if she could have commanded her feet to move, but dread turned every reflex, every nerve, every muscle to stone.

His eyes scanned the paper while his voice soothed his mount. "Easy, Samson, easy now."

Mr. Bingley, whom she had not noticed before, stopped abreast of Darcy, but his friend only waved in dismissal. "Go on, and I shall join you directly."

Bingley nodded and urged his horse forward, examining Elizabeth with drawn brows as he approached. "Good day, Miss Bennet." He tipped his hat.

Elizabeth glanced over her shoulder at his retreating form. Did she curtsey and greet him? She could not recall, riveted as she was by her poem in Darcy's hands. Apprehension quavered in her stomach. This was infinitely worse than explaining herself to her father. What had she been thinking to frame such fancies in ink?

There were not many lines that Darcy should linger long, yet he did. Elizabeth's fingers bunched and twisted her skirts. If only she could simply disappear!

Darcy's horse prodded him, the breeze stirring his black mane. His master rubbed the solid neck, crooning inarticulate sounds from deep in his throat.

When Darcy finally raised his head and peered toward Longbourn, Elizabeth strained to read his expression. Not bemused or scornful or angry, but pensive. He seemed lost in introspection, his stare unseeing. Her laughter bubbled inaudibly. To craft such verses and have him appear only thoughtful? What did she expect? He may have been the object, but not once did she conceive him as the reader.

His gaze retracted and snagged on her like fleece on a nail. Even across the expanse of twenty paces, the light that sparked in his eyes whenever they had crossed words ignited and spread, both dangerous and intriguing. He advanced, step by inexorable step, shadowed by his great beast, removing his riding gloves as he came.

Elizabeth held her breath, asphyxiated by anxiety. What would she say? How would she justify herself?

Darcy halted before her, closer than propriety sanctioned. His burning eyes explored her face like fingertips of dark flame stroking her cheeks, her forehead, her chin.

She exhaled her captive breath.

"I thought so." He stepped back and smiled.

She shook her head—something was amiss with her senses. Not once had he touched her. "Pardon me?"

He lifted the paper. "You wrote these."

"Yes." Fire crept from her neckline toward her temples.

"They are very pretty—or should I say *handsome*?" His lips twitched in a sardonic twist. He would say that. He was teasing her.

"You should not have read it, sir."

"You are correct, of course, and I ought to apologize, but I find that I cannot be sorry." He folded her paper and tucked it in his coat's left breast pocket.

She frowned. "You are impertinent, sir. You know full well that is my poetry, and you ought to return it."

"On the contrary, I believe I have some claim to it."
A chuckle rumbled from his chest. "But tell me, were
you hoping to drive away love or feed it?"

Elizabeth choked a little. To turn their passing banter
at Netherfield against her—insolent man! Even if he did
possess a pleasurable laugh, one she would not mind
hearing again.

Darcy stepped near, so near the warmth radiated from
his body.

She refused to withdraw.

"If you wish me to be impertinent"—his voice
dropped and his hands gripped her shoulders—"this is
impertinent."

His lips grazed hers like a flint struck in tinder, and
then they were ablaze: heat and light and fire for one
endless, dazzling moment. He released her, and the glow
flared in his eyes. She did not know whether to laugh or
cry or slap him, to chastise or beg him to kiss her again.

He caressed her cheek. "You are beautiful in your
confusion."

She could hardly hear for the rushing in her veins.

His mouth drew near her ear, his voice soft. "To read
such verses, Elizabeth, it stirs a man's heart. You must
know I return the sentiments."

Return her sentiments? What had she done? She
swallowed hard. "Indeed, until this moment, I had not an
idea of it."

Darcy straightened, both dark eyebrows climbing.
"Did you not?"

How could she confess the truth? Elizabeth dragged her lower lip between her teeth. She started the poem as a fanciful conjecture, a girlish whimsy, but the finished verses belied their genesis. She recast their every interaction, save the first, as if his impenetrable looks were not censure but approbation, received and reciprocated. Her words were effulgent with admiration and respect, passion and longing. But it was all an amusing fabrication.

She could never have envisioned an instance in which he would read it or, stranger still, that it would invite his addresses. Such had not been her intention—she had never desired his good opinion—but it flashed upon her with sudden, startling clarity, neither was his admiration unwelcome now that she gained it. The world pivoted on her answer.

"This is all so new," she stammered. "I think my pen admitted a truth I was unprepared to acknowledge." She touched his heart with quivering fingers where her poetry lay between them. "Perhaps you might consider these lines not so much a reflection of the present as a dream of what might be." Did disappointment flicker across his face? It was too fleeting to be certain.

"Then, in the interest of 'what might be,'" Darcy said, "I am compelled to correct the content of the first two lines."

Elizabeth arched an eyebrow. His presumption was bold, but considering the circumstances, she could hardly be offended.

His fingers rose as if to capture a windblown lock, but he lowered his arm and clasped her hand instead. His ungloved skin pressed warmth into her own. She trembled with the intimacy.

A hint of mirth tugged at the upraised corner of his mouth. "You *tempt* me almost beyond what I can bear, yet it is *intolerable* to be apart from you. And, while I am in *humor* to offer you the greatest *consequence*—"

Her eyes widened.

"—it is your words that have bestowed consequence upon me."

"That is a very pretty beginning, sir." She flushed in gratified embarrassment, for what she had written, for his words to her then and his words to her now. The capering wind gusted, and Elizabeth slipped her fingers from his grasp to wrap her arms against the chill.

"You must be cold." He offered his elbow. "Bingley wished to call and ask after Miss Bennet's health. Shall we join the others before our absence provokes comment?"

With her acquiescence, Darcy led them toward the house, his patient steed nudging his shoulder. They strolled in silence, and Elizabeth gazed up at him. He returned a gentle smile, content with the quiet. But her mind leapt ahead like a competitor in a foot race. When she dashed through the door on Lydia's tail, she never imagined her life might upend in a matter of minutes.

Near the front door, a waiting groom accepted the reins and led Darcy's horse away. Elizabeth bowed her head and tried to discipline her features in anticipation of meeting her family, but her lips demurred to obey. She watched her delicate slippers mount each step beside the steady tread of polished boots. Something quivered in her stomach.

Much remained to be learned, misunderstandings to resolve and apologies to exchange. Today was only a beginning. Darcy would request a courtship, for he had as good as declared himself—and she had as good as accepted. When Bingley held his ball, they would dance. Elizabeth failed to suppress a grin. No doubt Bingley was enamored with her beautiful elder sister. Perhaps the best friends would become brothers.

Lydia swung the front door wide. She must have been spying to shunt the servants from their duty.

"Lizzy, I see you caught Mr. Darcy." Her head tilted at a coquettish angle. "But did you catch your runaway verses?"

Never had Elizabeth felt so charitable toward her little sister, and she answered with perfect sincerity. "I am afraid they escaped my hands entirely."

Darcy only smiled.

# DARCY'S VERSION

Fitzwilliam Darcy rode down Meryton's main street beside Bingley, the local militia's red coats parting like a field of poppies before their horses.

"I cannot see why you insist on riding that beast." Bingley shook his head.

Samson tossed his black mane as if in offense. Darcy reached to rub his crest, not that his pedigreed animal required consolation. When he lifted his gaze, a familiar visage passed by. Darcy twisted around. Surely that was not his old nemesis? But the man had vanished, and Darcy dismissed the apparition with a shrug. He would not waste another thought on George Wickham.

"I mean," Bingley said, "there is no denying Samson's grand, but really, what is the value of a saddle horse too heavy for fences? And Comet could take him any day in a race."

Bingley's chestnut gelding swiveled his ears, anxious and alert. Darcy knew the breed well enough. After all, he kept a barn full of racing and hunting horses at Pemberley.

"If that were the only standard, you might be correct," Darcy said. "But I happen to like a horse I can trust not to land me in a ditch on the slightest provocation."

Bingley hooted. They both knew his Thoroughbred's volatility had unseated him more than once.

"In fact," Darcy grinned, "the knights of old chose Frisians for battle not only for their athleticism but also their docility."

"Fancy yourself a knight, do you? That means you must slay dragons and save damsels in distress"— Bingley chuckled—"which would require you to actually make yourself agreeable to the female population. I should like to see it."

Darcy grimaced at the unwelcome reminder of their errand. "We are en route to visit an entire house full of ladies. Surely, they are enough 'damsels' for even your taste. For my part, I want none of them." No matter how bewitching Miss Elizabeth nor how distressing her mother and younger sisters.

"That is readily apparent as you look every inch the dragon-slayer."

Mrs. Bennet's image materialized in Darcy's mind— they *were* bearding the she-dragon in her lair. "For which you should be glad. One of us must keep his head as you no doubt have already lost yours."

"I will not deny it." Bingley sighed. "Miss Bennet is the most beautiful angel I have ever beheld. But do you think she is well enough to receive me? Am I being too hasty in calling on her?"

"She was ill for a week under your own roof." Darcy rotated in the saddle. "She could have no objection to receiving you now."

"True, true." Bingley nodded, brow still furrowed. "But I would not wish to impose."

"I can assure you the Bennets will not consider your call an imposition." Darcy curbed a snort. As often as his friend was in love, he ought to have developed more confidence in the art.

They exited town onto the lane leading toward Longbourn, and Darcy appraised the Hertfordshire countryside. Gold-tipped limbs shivered in the breeze, and grassy hills undulated in verdant waves. The view appealed in its way, though it could not compare to Derbyshire's untamed splendor.

"In any event," Bingley said, "thank you for accompanying me."

"Of course." Darcy adjusted his reins, regretting his earlier sarcasm. Not that Bingley had an inkling of the exertion required. Seeing Miss Elizabeth was inevitable, but he resolved not to fix his eyes on her, in fact, not to attend her at all. She must be nothing to him.

They fell into easy conversation, but upon entering Longbourn's drive, Samson tucked his nose to his chest and commenced a half-pass, prancing laterally. Darcy twitched the reins and legged him into a straight line, but Samson's jitteriness persisted, each springy step jolting him in the saddle.

"I say," Bingley laughed, "the unflappable Samson is giving you the lie. I have never seen him so ruffled by a blustery day."

Neither had Darcy. Was a predator lurking in Longbourn's woods? A storm brewing? He looked up. A conflagration of colors cloaked nothing more alarming than the trees, and the sky shone clear cerulean. Was a mare nearby that Samson wished to impress? He almost laughed. Yes, and her name was Miss Elizabeth Bennet. Only Darcy's nerves were to blame for exciting his mount.

A rush of wind rattled through the leaves, bearing autumn's earthy scent and a white object streaking toward Samson's ears. The horse lurched sideways. Darcy kicked free of the stirrups and vaulted to the ground, intercepting the article in mid-air. He coaxed Samson to a semblance of calm and scanned for Bingley. His friend was halfway back to the lane, still wrestling the vicariously terrorized Comet into order. Darcy shook his head and chuckled, then turned his attention to the instigating object while he waited.

The short lines, blots, and strikethroughs suggested a sheet of drafted verses not yet transcribed. The hand was neither sloppy nor precise, yet distinctly feminine. He perused the first stanza, hoping to identify the author.

No <u>humor</u> to give <u>consequence</u>,
    no beauty to <u>tempt</u> you?
<u>Tolerable</u>, you called me,
    but you are proved untrue:

The words seemed strangely familiar. Perhaps it was the underlining. No matter. He folded the drivel to be returned unread, but then unfolded it to puzzle over the opening once more. *Tolerable*, his memory supplied the rest, *but not handsome enough to tempt me*. Disdain was quickly displaced by dismay. A flush crawled up his neck. Had Elizabeth overheard his intemperate remark at the Meryton Assembly? Were these her verses? Horrified by the irony and intensely curious, he read on.

> You think I have not noticed
>> the traitor in your eyes?
> He gives a merry chase;
>> he divulges your disguise.
>
> He savors all my speeches,
>> surrenders to my song,
> And presses me to dance with you—
>> dare me to be wrong—

Indeed, he did not dare. Clearly she was too quick to remark while he was too slow to suppress the interest he had shown. There was no stopping now. Bingley paused beside him, his presence irritating as a persistent fly. Darcy swatted the air, signaling with some impatience for his friend to continue.

Bingley sat immobile astride his mount.

Darcy lowered the paper to his side and glowered up into his friend's inquisitive countenance, his tone curt. "Go on, and I shall join you directly."

Bingley raised a brow but spurred his horse forward.

Darcy lifted the sheet, his eyes returning to the words with all the inexorability of autumn leaves to the ground.

He praises me for reading,
    admires me with his looks,
While you parry me with words
    and hide behind your books.

Invite me to your library,
    I'll linger there forever;
Amaze me with your gallantry,
    so noble, handsome, clever—

Speak to me with tenderness
    and to your lips I'll cling.
Forgive and live and love with me—
    let joy unending ring!

Darcy squinted at the concluding couplet, more disfigured by editorial markings than the rest, and slowed his pace to decipher each word. He inhaled a sharp breath and reread it.

Then dance me deeply, darkly down
    the cadence of desire,
And we will drown, swirling round
    a dazzling sea of fire.

His pulse thudded in every extremity. He would have loosened his neck cloth if he thought it would help. But the tightness was not of breath, it was of soul. It gripped him, closing around his heart with a fervency that bordered on pain. Her words would not release him. He read them again and again until Samson nuzzled him back to reality. Good horse. He scratched the proffered neck, murmuring to him from long habit, and regarded the paper in his hand. Heavens above, what a woman!

Darcy slowly raised his head and looked toward Longbourn, still obscured by a turn in the drive. Elizabeth was there, somewhere in those rooms, her sparkling eyes and playful manners concealing an undertow of passion. How would he sit across from her and before all her family or, heaven forbid, near her in perfect politeness when heart called to heart and deep called to deep?

He had never run from a fight, but until now he had never faced a fight he could not win. If he did not leave, flee to Netherfield and on to London, he was lost. He was a fool to believe he could resist her. He had chained his perfidious heart with the firmest resolve, that strength of character for which he was renowned, but her words melted his bonds as easily as wax.

What cared he for inferior connections when there was such a woman in the world who loved him? Except he did care. Very much. Perhaps too much. But really, would offering for her be spurning duty and casting off honor? He stared into the distance and thwacked Samson's reins against his thigh, then traced the drive as if a solution would trot round the bend.

A golden shimmer in the foreground of his vision shifted his focus. Elizabeth. How long had she been standing there? Her gown snapped about her legs like a slackened sail, the wind silhouetting her sprightly curves in billowing muslin and shaping her exposed locks into a dark halo. She remained exquisitely still. Even twenty yards distant, anxiety clouded her normally bright features.

Darcy's eyes trapped hers, willing her to wait as he crossed the chasm between them. Hooves clomped behind him, crunching the gravel. He must touch her, but he would not sully her skin with Samson's sweat. He stripped off his riding gloves and tucked them at his waist, propriety be hanged.

He stopped a hands-breadth from her and examined her upturned face. The rich brown eyes searching his that could shine with compassion and wit and anger. The smooth forehead but a stage for those achingly expressive brows. The impudent nose still doused with late summer freckles. Her exhalation enveloped him and he retreated a step, heady with her scent. Any doubts about her authorship were cast aside.

He smiled. "I thought so."

"Pardon me?"

Darcy gestured with her verses. "You wrote these."

A violent blush confirmed his conjecture, and her discomposure lent him the advantage.

"They are very pretty," he smirked, "or should I say handsome?"

"You should not have read it, sir." Her brows pinched together.

He appreciated her indignation as well as her modesty. While he was gratified to have inspired this degree of fervor, she would have been extremely improper to compose such a private poem for him—though now that he possessed it, he had no intention of yielding.

Samson whickered and, thrusting his whiskered muzzle between them, nipped at the paper. Nosy animal. Darcy shoved the huge head behind his back, then creased the poem with care and secreted it close to his heart.

Elizabeth's glittering eyes followed every movement.

"You are correct, of course," he said, "and I ought to apologize, but I find that I cannot be sorry."

"You are impertinent, sir. You know full well that is my poetry and you ought to return it." Her eyes sparked and an eyebrow quirked in her usual teasing fashion, inciting him to respond in kind.

"On the contrary, I believe I have some claim to it. But tell me, were you hoping to drive away love or feed it?"

Elizabeth cleared her throat, her lips parting and then pursing, their movement utterly beguiling. *Dance me deeply* thundered in his ears like a summons. Before she could speak, he stepped from the chill of the day into the heat of her proximity.

"If you wish me to be impertinent"—he grasped her shoulders and the connection seared up his arms—"this is impertinent." Then his lips were dancing with hers, and he was lost to the intoxicating rhythm, drowning in a molten sea, swept to the precipice of a depthless vortex.

He withdrew, every sense aflame. He gasped for air and sought to gauge her reaction. A flurry of unreadable emotion flashed through her eyes before she glanced aside. Doubtless his ardor frightened her, a maiden unkissed.

"You are beautiful in your confusion." He stroked her cheek, whispering the truth. "To read such verses, Elizabeth, it stirs a man's heart. You must know I return the sentiments."

Her breath tickled his ear and tingled down his spine. "Indeed, until this moment, I had not an idea of it."

He reared back, searching her face for answers, hoping he misheard. "Did you not?"

Elizabeth bit her lip, and her forehead wrinkled. The throbbing in his veins measured each second of dreadful silence. Samson snorted against his back in sympathy.

"This is all so new." Her answer floated out, breathless and halting. "I think my pen admitted a truth I was unprepared to acknowledge." She rested her palm on his lapel, and his chest expanded under the contact. "Perhaps you might consider these lines not so much a reflection of the present as a dream of what might be."

How could she have written such lines if she did not mean them? Darcy flailed to comprehend her assertion, bewilderment extinguishing the last embers of passion. A tiny voice advocated escape. Surely it was all a grave misunderstanding. His heart protested—to turn back now, when in addition to her manifold attributes, he had glimpsed her fiery depths? How could he? If her verses were not what he thought, not what he hoped, at least they were a start and that must suffice.

"Then in the interest of 'what might be,' I am compelled to correct the content of the first two lines." Sunlight glinting in her hair beckoned his touch, but he settled for taking her hand, smooth and cool between his. "You tempt me almost beyond what I can bear, yet it is intolerable to be apart from you. And, while I am in humor to offer you the greatest consequence, it is your words that have bestowed consequence upon me."

"That is a very pretty beginning, sir." Humor twinkled in her tone. Her ebony lashes, so long and fine, lowered against her rosy cheeks, begging to be kissed.

The wind picked up, causing her to shiver and chafe her upper arms for warmth—and no wonder, for she was without a wrap. He offered to escort her inside and she accepted.

A perfect contentment settled over him with Elizabeth on one elbow, her eyes seeking his and glowing once more, and Samson's muzzle bumping his other shoulder. His uncomplaining steed had stood by him through the whole, as faithful a charger as any knight and his damsel could wish. Bring on the dragon. Darcy cleared his throat to conceal a chuckle. When they neared the house and a servant conducted Samson toward the stables, Darcy gave the broad, black rump an affectionate pat.

The front door flew open, framing Elizabeth's youngest sister in all her vulgarity, yet her saucy manner betrayed a family resemblance. "Lizzy, I see you caught Mr. Darcy, but did you catch your runaway verses?"

Elizabeth's voice was steady. "I am afraid they escaped my hands entirely."

Darcy smiled, for her verses fluttered within his coat, her heart beating in cadence with his own.

.

# NEITHER SLUMBER NOR SLEEP

A splendid old home in the north of England luxuriates in the afternoon sun, aglow with enticing luminosity. Countless visitors pass through its gates to admire the stonework, marvel over the elegant rooms, and wander the extensive park in search of the best prospects. Beyond the shimmering lake, with its well-trod tracks and sheltered glades, rises a little-regarded prominence topped by a weathered bench.

The commanding view encompasses not only the gracefully situated structure, tree-strewn lawns, and rich fields spreading across and down the valley, but also the woodlands which cloak the mounting hills and draw the eye upward to the majestic peaks. In good light, those who know to look may discern the inscription on the bench's tarnished plate. This is its story.

# PRELUDE

The Reverend William Collins puffed out his chest and surveyed the burnished length of Rosings' dinner table, spread this fine autumn night with a sumptuous palette of seasonal delicacies. How good and pleasant was the beneficence of such a patroness!

"So Miss Bennet and Mr. Bingley are to be wed." Lady Catherine pried another bite of meat from the delicate quail. "It is a most advantageous match for her."

Mr. Collins cleared his throat. "I could not agree more, your ladyship, and—"

"One cannot begrudge her any mercenary tactics," she spoke over him, "considering how small her portion is."

"No, of course not." Collins nodded and glanced at his wife. In her presence, it would not do to mention that such motives would have been unnecessary had Miss Elizabeth seen fit to accept his initial offer of marriage.

"When is the wedding to be?"

"In January, ma'am, although the precise date is not yet fixed," Charlotte said.

"I suppose you will consider it prudent to attend."

"We could not possibly—" Collins started to disclaim.

"Naturally. It is only right as the heir presumptive that you should lend your support to the eldest Bennet's nuptials. Not to mention the Bingleys will be your future neighbors. One cannot give too much forethought to these matters."

Collins nodded with such rapidity that his vision blurred.

"I shall grant you leave to extend your trip for a fortnight, so that Mrs. Collins may take advantage of your travels to enjoy a lengthier visit with family. But mind you do not miss more than one Sunday."

"How kind of you. We shall be pleased to accept." Charlotte's voice came from Collins' right. The conversation was proceeding too swiftly for him.

"What forbearance and understanding with which you continually grace us, madam," Collins said, warming to his gratitude, "to allow—"

"Yes, yes," she waggled knobby fingers at him, her rings glinting in the candlelight, "and have you any other news from Hertfordshire?"

Though Lady Catherine had spoken to his wife, Collins was confident he could answer. "As a matter of fact, it seems the felicitations of one wedding have ignited rumor of a second."

Charlotte inexplicably trod on his foot. He yelped.

"Mr. Collins," Lady Catherine said, "it is not necessary to embroider your tale with dramatics. A direct account will suffice."

"What my husband intends to convey," Charlotte smiled, "is that Miss Bingley is eager to find a husband now that she will no longer be keeping house for her brother."

"That is not at all what I meant to say," Collins countered.

"Well, I cannot imagine she shall find one in Hertfordshire," Lady Catherine said. "Miss Bingley had better remove to London for the Season."

"I meant—ouch!" Collins swallowed a second shriek as Charlotte stomped on his sore foot.

"Mr. Collins wishes to express that Miss Bingley's residence is in London already, on Grosvenor Street as we have been given to understand."

While Lady Catherine expounded on the comparative worth of various London neighborhoods, Collins leveled a look at his wife intended to halt her exceedingly odd conduct. Charlotte pressed her lips closed and contemplated the creased linen in her lap. That was better.

When Lady Catherine concluded her speech, Collins seized the opening.

"I know nothing of Miss Bingley's marital aspirations," he said, making his third attempt, "but my cousin, Miss Elizabeth—" The pain in his instep was so excruciating that he nearly howled. What did Charlotte mean by accosting him in this fashion and under their patroness' table, no less? He would condemn her inappropriate behavior in the sharpest terms once they returned to their own abode.

"I recommend betony syrup to ease sour belching, Mr. Collins. You may see Parker to provision you with a dose or two," Lady Catherine said. "Or a hot bag of caraway seed placed on the lower abdomen, if the syrup is ineffectual."

He blinked at her. He did not have a stomach ailment.

"You may be excused from the table immediately lest your outbursts likewise afflict me with indigestion." She flicked both hands at him in dismissal.

"Please accept my most abject apologies, your ladyship," he pleaded in an agony of contrition, rising from his seat in obedience while rushing to deliver his report. "But you must overlook Mrs. Collins' ill-timed remarks, for I referred to rumors of an alliance between my own cousin, Miss Elizabeth Bennet, and your illustrious nephew, Mr. Darcy. This spurious allusion is no doubt the product of fanciful invention and—"

"What?" Lady Catherine bellowed, exposing a mouthful of partially masticated fowl. Her generous bosoms rolled like the galloping haunches of a horse.

Collins' eyes went wide at the unanticipated effect. Perhaps he should flee the room under the convenient pretense of indigestion, but that was beneath his dignity as a clergyman. He resumed his seat.

"To be sure, everyone knows Mr. Darcy is destined for your own fair daughter," he said, hoping to appease her, "and none could begin to rival her attractions in his eyes."

A glance showed him the young lady in question sitting agog in witness to the spectacle and quite as pale as her mother was crimson.

"That Darcy should offer for that scheming upstart, that ungrateful country nobody with her insolent manners and alluring eyes? It is impossible." Lady Catherine's volume every instant increased alongside her color. She belabored her objections for what seemed a quarter hour.

Collins slid lower in his chair, for once wishing he were neither such a tall, robust fellow nor any relation of the Bennets.

Veins bulging at her temples, Lady Catherine choked out her final decree, the words muffled through a froth of spittle. "I… for…bid… it."

"Please, I beg you with all earnestness, madam, you must calm yourself," Charlotte asserted at the first possible interlude. "You must not credit what is merely hearsay. Mr. Collins speaks of rumor only."

But Lady Catherine's face had deepened from red to violet, and her great bejeweled fingers were clutching at her throat. She gasped for breath that would not come, toppled forward, and expired. Her aquiline nose came to rest on a pillow of peas and potatoes, and a coronet of quail bones crowned her noble brow.

Mr. Collins had never seen a dinner plate addressed with such condescension or graciousness.

# FUGUE

*Late December 1812, London*

A draught snaked through the sheltering buildings and buffeted the London street. It snagged Elizabeth's pelisse and, despite their brisk pace, made the thick fabric cling to her legs with all the persistence of a shy child. She shivered.

"You are not chilled, are you?" Jane peered across their linked arms.

"No more than you." Elizabeth offered a bright smile and bumped her sister's shoulder. "The joy of this expedition and the company of my sisters afford all the warmth I need." They were on their final errand for Jane's wedding clothes, and though Elizabeth would not confess aloud that she was tiring, neither would she allow a little cold to dampen her spirits. What a happy contrast to last year, when Jane's London sojourn deflated all their expectations of Mr. Bingley.

Jane halted near the steps to an unfamiliar church and withdrew her arm. "Lizzy, I would not in any way jeopardize your health. You are only just free of the sickroom."

"You need not be concerned. My aunt and uncle are the most agreeable and conscientious hosts, but I could not bear being shut in another day." Had she not already spent six of the past ten in her bed, including Christmas?

Ah, well, such was the price of disregarding her mother's objections and romping with her sniffling little cousins.

Kitty and Mary had caught up to their elder sisters and were following the conversation with swiveling bonnets.

"Do you not agree it is a perfect day in Christmastide?" Elizabeth said, wishing to change the topic. "The breeze has cleared all the haze."

If she closed her eyes to the grimy city and angled her face to the afternoon sun, she could almost imagine herself on a Hertfordshire lane. She inhaled and the next second wished she had not. Crisp air seared down her throat and convulsed her lungs. A wracking cough stooped her. Hands rubbed her back and her coughing abated, but a hushed dispute broke out above her bowed head. Did they think she could not hear just because she could not breathe?

Jane's voice emerged over the others' protests. "That clinches it. We are taking Lizzy home. I will hear no argument."

Elizabeth cleared her throat several times, straightened, and gestured behind her. "There is no need for such haste, not when we are already arrived. I might rest in this church while you finish."

"I would be happy to keep Lizzy company," added Mary.

Jane began to object.

"Of course you would." Kitty rolled her eyes at Mary. "We are all aware how much *you* delight in shopping."

Elizabeth stepped back and slipped her hand through Mary's elbow. "See, it is arranged to everyone's satisfaction."

"Not to mine," Jane said.

"Please?" Kitty seized her eldest sister's gloved fingers and tugged her toward the shops. "We should go now while the patterns are fresh in our minds. The modiste wanted the trimmings immediately, if she is to complete the remaining gowns before we leave Town and return to Longbourn."

Jane shook her head, setting golden curls swinging against rosy cheeks, but she was wavering. The moment was to Elizabeth's advantage.

"Kitty is right," Elizabeth pressed, "you know she is. You two continue on. Mary and I shall be fine, truly, and will look forward to a detailed account of your purchases and orders."

Mary made a strangled noise but fell short of voicing her displeasure with that prospect.

"It would be convenient to conclude today." Jane sighed. "If you are certain?"

"Completely certain." Elizabeth masked another cough with a laugh, and the foursome arranged to reconvene at the church in two hours.

\*\*\*\*\*

The granite steps were not especially numerous or steep, but Elizabeth was winded by the time they reached the broad double doors.

"From the manner in which you were leaning on me," Mary said, "are you certain we should not call for the carriage and return to the Gardiners? No one would mind, least of all Jane."

"That is good of you, but I am only fatigued from too many days of inactivity. Resting in a pew for a short while should set me to rights."

One oaken door creaked as they opened it and stole into the cool, dim narthex.

Mary sniffed. "Can you smell that?"

Elizabeth could, which was a welcome change. "Evergreen boughs and something sweet?"

"Frankincense, I think. Perhaps it is part of the High Church revival."

"I could not say." In truth, Elizabeth did not care. Now that relief was within sight, she desired only to sit. Sunlight streamed through the clerestory windows, bathing half the sanctuary in an inviting glow that at least gave an illusion of warmth. She slid into the first available pew and wilted against the rigid bench.

Mary stopped nearby and rotated to examine her surroundings. "You would not mind if I looked about, would you?"

Elizabeth scanned the edifice. It boasted statuary near the walls and an ornate chancel screen at the front.

Indeed, a striking disparity from their plain little church in Meryton or even the Gardiners' larger but equally plain church in Cheapside. Her sister's initial assessment was likely correct. Mary should know, given her familiarity with Alexander Knox' writings and her fascination with the budding resurgence in pre-Reformation worship.

"I should not mind at all," Elizabeth said. "Please take your time."

Mary moved away.

Elizabeth slouched until she could support her neck against the upright back. No one would term it comfortable, and it was certainly not designed to encourage sleep, but at least she could rest.

Her eyes traveled up to the dust particles floating on the sunlight. They swirled in a glittering dance that reminded her of the beautiful gowns, the merriment, and the gentlemen who had partnered her. Nor was it strange that her next thought should be of Mr. Darcy, whom she had not seen since his visit to Longbourn in September. He was coming to the wedding to stand up with his friend as Elizabeth would stand up with Jane.

But would the awkwardness that marked their last encounter still prevail? For a time, she hoped Darcy might return to Netherfield, until Lady Catherine died and he was much occupied with his aunt's and cousin's affairs. Or at least that was what Bingley reported in his distracted manner and Charlotte confirmed in her letters. Although Elizabeth confessed her feelings to Jane, who kept nothing from her betrothed, Elizabeth was obliged to conclude that either Bingley had been unusually circumspect with his friend, or she had been wrong in thinking it within her power to reawaken Darcy's affections. Otherwise, Darcy would have come.

None of that mattered now. She would meet him in a matter of weeks, and finding an occasion to express her gratitude was paramount.

"I have made a discovery!"

Elizabeth started at Mary's excited voice. "Has the rector got into the wine?"

Mary grimaced her disapproval. "There is a small museum adjacent to the church and dedicated to its history. This structure is the third to stand on this site." Mary indicated an archway under which a matron in mobcap and fichu stood observing them. "The docent is kind enough to grant me a tour, but I did not wish to abandon you."

"Take your pleasure." Elizabeth waved an acknowledgement to the older woman. "I am glad for further respite."

Mary smiled with more true warmth than Elizabeth had seen from her in an age.

Elizabeth turned toward the chancel. Sunlight shone through the screen's rich wood and dappled the altar in white, like peering through a veil into the holy of holies, as if God Himself were loitering with her. Or the reverse. This was His house after all. A soft smile tugged at her lips. Even isolated by sickness, she was not shielded from the hubbub of twelve family members under one roof. Was it not a gift, these quiet moments to reflect on the end of one year and the beginning of another?

The thought inspired her gratitude—and she had much for which to be grateful. Jane's heartache turned to elation when Bingley returned and professed his love. Elizabeth could thank Darcy for that. Lydia was married and settled with Wickham in his Newcastle regiment. The circumstances were far from ideal, but it could have been much worse. She could thank Darcy for that as well.

She was grateful to have visited Pemberley in the summer, to witness for herself how Darcy had changed and how she misunderstood him. She liked to believe she too had grown humbler and more generous in her judgments. For that also she must credit Darcy. A laugh escaped and reverberated from the vaulted ceiling. Thank the good Lord for bringing Mr. Darcy into her life, but was there nothing that did not circle back to him?

Elizabeth cast about for a moment and thought of Charlotte. Her dear friend was content as she could be in her situation and keen to welcome the consolation of baby Collins. Darcy could not claim a role in that, though it did stir recollections of his proposal at Hunsford. The offense of his opinions had long since faded in her memory, and she recalled only his impassioned declaration. It must be approaching six months since gratitude for his affections first overwhelmed her—affections she might have returned. But she had disciplined her mind to avoid such speculation, and she would not change her habit now. Nothing was to be gained in dwelling on what might have been.

Instead, Elizabeth reclined again, closed her eyes, and prayed for Darcy—prayed the Lord might favor him as He had her, that he would find joy and fulfillment in the coming year. That done, she forced her thoughts into a different course, giving thanks one by one for the prior year's blessings, until the gratitude swelled in her heart with palpable warmth and no words remained.

*****

Soft footfalls stirred Elizabeth from her repose. Mary must have come to check on her, since she doubted having slept long enough for Jane to complete her shopping and return. And Kitty had never measured up to the stealth of her pet name.

An impish idea flitted through Elizabeth's mind, and she bit back a smile. Yes, she did dare. Years had passed since they played such a childish game, but the very unexpectedness could only make it more effective. Besides, Mary would benefit from a healthy bout of laughter.

The footsteps continued. One quiet heel click followed by another until, coming even with her pew, they halted.

Elizabeth waited in perfect stillness, forcing herself to feign sleep and heighten the suspense until she could delay no longer.

"The bed's mine," she exclaimed, opening her eyes and thrusting her hands in the air all at once.

Her observer leapt backwards and collided with the opposite pew. Black clad arms and legs wheeled like a windmill. Unable to regain his footing, the man capsized, and she was regaled with his upturned soles.

"Oh, I am so sorry, sir." Elizabeth jumped up and crossed the aisle, already framing her apologies to the rector. "Are you hurt?"

The dark eyes of none other than Mr. Fitzwilliam Darcy stared at her from his recumbent position on the pew bench. He shoved himself to his elbows. "Miss Bennet!"

She curtseyed but did not know where to look. If the heat in her cheeks was any indication, all her blood must have rushed to her face. Of every possible manner in which she might have encountered him, why must she succumb to a juvenile whim at such a moment?

"Forgive me for not greeting you properly," he said, "but I find myself momentarily indisposed."

She forced herself to look at him. His pose was so undignified, reclining with knees elevated over the pew's end, that were she not overwhelmed by mortification, guilt and shock, she might have laughed. "Er... May I assist you?"

He considered her for a moment and smiled, but did not accept her outstretched hand. His legs found the floor in a smooth motion and he stood. Her eyes followed his face until she was forced to angle her head back. She had forgotten precisely how tall he was. Or how handsome.

"I did not realize you were in Town, sir. Mr. Bingley said you were keeping Christmas in Kent this year."

"Yes," he smiled, "we did and are only recently arrived. I did not wish Anne to be alone for her first Christmas without her mother, and she was not strong enough to travel here."

"How very thoughtful," Elizabeth said, struck by the fondness and consideration with which Darcy mentioned Miss de Bourgh. Why had it never occurred to her that more than cousinly concern might have kept him in Kent? "May I extend belated condolences for your aunt's death?"

"Thank you." He gestured to the pew she recently vacated, clearly wishing an end to the prior subject. "I was making every effort to tread softly and not disrupt your prayers, but..."

"Oh, I was not praying. I mean, I was praying before, but just then I was—" How could she explain?

"Lying in wait for unsuspecting churchgoers?"

"No. Yes. For my sister anyway, you see—" She laughed despite her embarrassment. "I only meant to surprise her with a very silly game we devised in our girlhood."

"That will not do at all." He shook his head. "I require a better explanation for being compelled to such an indignity."

She could not decide if he was humored or offended. "In which case I am afraid I must disappoint you, sir, as a better explanation does not exist."

"Come, Miss Bennet, you may at least acquaint me with the particulars of how this game is played."

"If you wish, but it is of no consequence."

The corners of his eyes creased. "Your resistance has aroused my curiosity."

"It was very silly. Once the lights were put out, Jane and I, being the eldest, would feign sleep, and the younger girls would try to sneak into our beds without alerting us to their presence. If we heard them, then we would call out 'the bed's mine.'"

"And if you did not apprehend the intruder?"

"Then I was obliged to share my bed for the night." She shrugged. "You see, sir, it was only a simple folly among children."

He leaned forward and lowered his voice. "An entertaining pastime, to be sure, and I will even admit to playing any number of games with my cousins as a youth, but might I suggest you reserve such amusements for the privacy of your home?"

She flushed yet again. "Be assured that we have outgrown such diversions."

"So I see." A fleeting smirk pulled at his lips before he glanced around the sanctuary. "Perhaps we might continue this conversation elsewhere, lest the rector dismiss us from the premises for irreverence."

"I would like that," she said, "but I am to await my sisters here."

"The church's garden offers a labyrinth which we might explore." He indicated that she precede him. "That is, if you do not find the day too cool."

How fortunate that her earlier weariness had all but vanished. "It sounds perfect."

*****

"Lizzy, you must see this." Mary bent over a display, her bonnet ribbons trailing on the case. Her fingers beckoned toward Elizabeth although she had yet to lift her gaze.

Elizabeth cast Darcy an apologetic glance as she complied.

"It is a letter scribed by Lancelot Andrewes himself." Mary straightened. "Oh. Mr. Darcy. I did not observe you there."

Elizabeth's eyes traveled between them, curious to gauge Darcy's response.

"Miss Mary." He bowed. "It is a pleasure to see you again."

Mary removed her spectacles but seemed at a loss for reply.

"Mr. Darcy happened upon me while also seeking respite from escorting his sister and her companion on a shopping expedition. We were thinking to refresh ourselves with a turn in the labyrinth." Elizabeth indicated the modest garden. From the window, she could just make out the back of a wooden bench peeking above the patterned hedge rows. "Would you care to join us?"

Mary glanced between the letter and Darcy, then back to Elizabeth. "Do you think it wise, especially since—"

"You need not, if you prefer to stay. You may observe us from here." Elizabeth interrupted, wishing to preclude any mention of her health. "And Jane and Kitty shall come to fetch us within the hour."

"So soon?" Mary stroked the volumes on a nearby shelf. "But they have all the Caroline Divines."

"Then it is settled," Darcy said. "Should you need us, we shall be within sight."

With one hand under Elizabeth's elbow, Darcy directed her to the door. The docent intercepted them, declaiming that the garden was much neglected and scheduled for renovations in the spring, but Darcy assured her it was perfectly adequate and assisted Elizabeth down several steps to the path. They strolled between the low hedges in wordless companionship, stones crunching beneath their shoes and the racket of pattens, hooves, and carriage wheels echoing in their ears.

The wind seemed frigid after the church's comparative warmth. Elizabeth folded her arms across her chest and took shallow breaths in an effort to avoid coughing, but her throat tickled and she was obliged to produce her handkerchief.

Darcy stopped and studied her. "May I enquire if you have been ill?"

"A trifling cold, nothing to warrant concern, and I am on the mend."

"Then we ought not expose you to the winter air. Allow me to return you inside."

"No, please." She rested her fingers on his sleeve. "I have been caged within doors far too long."

"An unkempt garden is a poor substitute for a ramble in the country. Really, Miss Bennet, I insist."

"Mr. Darcy." She pressed his arm. "There is something about which I would speak with you, if we might tarry a few minutes."

He glanced at her fingers. "Certainly whatever you have to say may be said as well within doors."

"We have a singular opportunity for privacy, and I will not take long." If she might avail herself of this opening to express her gratitude, then that at least would not be weighing upon her during Jane's wedding festivities.

His brow creased in deliberation, but she remained firm in her resolve.

"Very well," he said, "but I will hold you to your brevity."

He tucked her arm into his and navigated further into the winding route, the pattern proving more maze than labyrinth. Overgrown branches snatched at their legs, but the shrubs were no taller than her waist. Since the garden was narrow, they made swift progress toward the bench on the far side.

When they emerged, Darcy shoved the weather-worn wooden frame with a finger, and it responded with a creak. A discolored brass plate bore the faded inscription "Psalm 121."

"Pardon the incivility, but permit me to test its sturdiness before I seat you." Darcy lowered himself gingerly.

Elizabeth did not wait for him to complete his assessment and installed herself on the opposite side. The bench rocked sideways with a squeak.

She giggled. "Is it not rustic and charming?"

"I will not deign to humor that comment with a reply," he said, though there was nothing of arrogance and much of amusement in his voice. "Now, what is so important that you must risk your health to tell me?"

She folded her hands in her lap and swallowed. Why must it be difficult to frame words she had rehearsed over many months? "What I have to say is terribly overdue. You must understand I had been hoping to speak with you when you came into Hertfordshire last autumn, but you were called away to Kent before we were afforded an opportunity."

His brows knit. "Settling Lady Catherine's estate has certainly taken far longer than I anticipated. My aunt named me her executor because she anticipated— Well, never mind that. But were you expecting me to return into Hertfordshire?"

"Not expected—not exactly," her eyes dropped to the untended grass underfoot, "more like hoped."

"Truly, Miss Bennet?"

She nodded and lifted her gaze. He was searching her face, though she did not know to what end. But she could not allow his earnest scrutiny to distract her from her purpose. "Oh, but Mr. Darcy, this is not what I wished to say."

"Is it not?"

"No." Now was the moment. She must see her object to its conclusion. "I wish to express my appreciation to you, inadequate though words must be, for reuniting Jane and Bingley and, more importantly, for what you sacrificed in rescuing Lydia. If my family were aware of all you have done, my thanks would be multiplied fivefold, but as they are not, please accept my sincere gratitude on their behalf."

"Ah." He leaned back. The bench groaned in response. "This is why you hoped I would return, so that you might thank me?"

"Yes." That and more, but she could hardly confess as much.

"My actions were never intended to come to your notice. I am sorry that they have and that it has caused

you unease. Please do not distress yourself any longer."
He offered a tight smile. "You are sufficiently
acquainted with my history with Wickham to understand
that I felt a degree of responsibility in being the means
that allowed him to prey on your sister."

"It was not your fault."

"Do not attempt to acquit me." He raised a hand. "I
had other, stronger motivations as well."

"I know," she said before he could elaborate. At least
she could exploit this chance to prove his virtues had not
gone unnoticed. "Your character and integrity, your
scrupulous application of principle have long held my
respect."

"I am honored by your compliments." His brow drew
down.

If he was honored, then why did he appear the
opposite? Before she could determine how to respond,
he continued.

"It may have been the correct and moral course, but
you must not credit me for any such pure motives." His
mouth opened and then closed before he spoke. "I
believe I thought only of you."

She moistened her lips. Was it possible he still cared
for her? She had wondered as much at Pemberley, but he
was so very reserved when he returned to Longbourn
and now all these months had passed. Silence ensued,
but she felt she must speak. "Mr. Darcy, I—I—"

"Miss Bennet—Elizabeth," he slid closer on the
bench and it grumbled under his shifting weight, "I

realize that close to a year has elapsed since my confession last April, but my feelings, my wishes are unchanged." He stretched for her hand where it was clutched tightly in her other.

She gazed at him in wonderment and met his fingers with her own.

He scooted closer. The bench complained. "But if you still feel—"

Splitting wood exploded in her ears, and she lurched sideways. Her head thudded into the earth. An impossible weight landed atop her, driving her back into something sharp and unyielding. She felt dizzy and out of breath and closed her eyes.

Darcy's weight crushed against the length of her, and his hat's scratchy felt lodged beneath her chin. The vibration against her chest told her he was speaking, but his words were muffled and his struggles forced all remaining air from her lungs. He continued to shift about until the pressure eased somewhat.

She gasped and turned her head aside to cough.

"Elizabeth!" Anxiety riddled his voice. "Are you injured?"

A peculiar lethargy made it difficult to lift her lids. When she did, she first saw a withered vine clinging to the stone wall directly in her field of vision. How did something so fragile manage to climb the impervious surface?

"Elizabeth, please." Darcy recalled her. "Can you answer me?"

She took a shallow breath and rotated her head toward him. He had wedged one arm near her shoulder and lifted his head from her torso, but still she started at the nearness of his face, so near she could distinguish the dark points of whiskers peppering his skin and delicate vessels reddening with strain. His lips moved.

She heard the words, but their sense came slowly, like translating Italian at the opera.

"Are you hurt?" he repeated.

His eyes were— Had she ever truly looked into his eyes?

"Miss Bennet, this is most distressing."

"I am well," she said at last, though omitting to mention the discomfort from the armrest beneath her back, "only a little out of breath."

"I do apologize, but I cannot"—he struggled again—"free myself. Can you see what is pinning me against you?"

"I will try," she said.

Her stomach contracted beneath him until she could raise her head enough to assess the problem. His cheek was warm and coarse against hers, and the musky oils in his hair tantalized her nose. She sank back, exhausted from the effort and dismayed by her traitorous senses.

"Well?" Darcy prompted after a moment.

"We are akin to beef in one of the earl's infamous sandwiches."

Darcy frowned. "This is hardly the time to jest."

"I thought a mental picture might prove useful." She sighed. "My armrest gave way and, along with the seat, now lies beneath me like the bottom slice of toast. The back of the bench collapsed forward and is resting on you like the top slice of toast."

"But that does not explain why I cannot dislodge it."

"Ah, you forget the other armrest. The angle made it difficult to discern, but your armrest appears to have fallen across the back of the bench such that it is acting as a lock."

He nodded. "If I can gain another inch or so, perhaps you might be able to wriggle out."

He fought against the trap and though she tried to comply, in her weakened state and beneath his substantial bulk, she could not make any progress. The effort induced another coughing fit.

When she recovered her breath, she said, "I am sorry, but I am afraid I cannot move either."

He was flushed with embarrassment and exertion, but he relaxed his efforts and considered her. "You must not try again, Miss Bennet. It is too much strain after your illness."

She swallowed a teasing comment. He meant to be considerate, she knew he did, but the strain of bearing nearly his full weight was not insignificant.

He was studying her with great solemnity, in all likelihood evaluating every possible solution, but the incongruity between his serious appraisal and their improbable dilemma suddenly struck her. She pressed her lips together.

"No," he said, "you would not dare laugh."

Her cheeks quivered and she tried to restrain herself, but a hiccup of humor slipped out and then another. Laughter shook her body and him by proximity.

He closed his eyes and exhaled a long, slow breath before opening them again. "Please, Miss Bennet. You must stop."

"Even you must admit the absurdity of our situation." She managed at last to quiet her giggles. "If you cannot laugh in moments like these, then what can you do?"

"I have never had a moment like this."

That made her laugh again. "Then what do you propose?"

He did not answer, his gaze instead caressing her features, his eyes pausing on her brow or her lips or her cheek, eyes as rich and warm as the coffee lingering on his breath. Perception of his nearness, of his person pressing into her, overcame all thought of escape.

"Your eyes are"—his voice rumbled against her—"I always thought your eyes very fine, but I never realized how…" His words trailed off.

Did he mean to kiss her? Surely such a gentleman would never take advantage of a lady in a compromised position. Her heart began to pound. His eyes flicked to hers in recognition. How extraordinary! He could sense her heart beating. She concentrated and likewise discerned the rhythm of his heart, drumming with equal rapidity. The arm that supported him began to tremble, and the comic aspect of their quandary evaporated.

"Forgive me." He sighed. "I regret the further imposition, but I think the only escape is if—" His ruddiness deepened.

"Yes, Mr. Darcy?"

"If I allow my full weight to rest on you, then the pressure on the bench should ease and I may be able to roll free."

"Like the proverbial fist in the jar?" She attempted a light tone.

"Precisely." He paused and when he spoke again, his voice was quiet. "It will help if you do not resist."

Comprehension of his request broke over her. He wished her to release the tension in her muscles, to willingly receive his added weight that she might aid in diminishing their profile. As if their current intimacy were insufficient.

She sighed even as her heart began to hammer. "Very well."

Her head lolled sideways to comply, and the change in angle carried with it the sound of voices. "Wait. Do you hear that?"

He too inclined his head to listen. "I would rather not be found in such a predicament."

"You think I would?"

"The voices are female. I imagine they are your sisters."

Elizabeth listened once more, but the wind distorted the sound too much to be confident. "It could just as well be your sister and her companion."

A horrified expression crossed his face. "Quickly, Miss Bennet."

She turned her head aside again, exhaling and flattening herself as much as the bench arm beneath her would allow. He dropped against her and grunted with the strain of rolling free. She endeavored to ignore the alarming sensations this produced.

"Brother!" A voice high and clear with dismay halted his efforts.

Darcy raised himself as much as he could and looked up. He groaned. "Georgiana. The bench collapsed and we are—"

Elizabeth tilted her head back and saw Miss Darcy upside down, her eyes round and mouth agape.

"Miss Elizabeth!" She exclaimed.

"—trapped," concluded Darcy.

"Oh!" Miss Darcy rushed toward the bench. "Let me help."

"The right-hand arm," directed Darcy, "it must be released."

Elizabeth could not see what Miss Darcy was doing, but the far end of the bench rose. Darcy inched forward, catching himself on elbows to either side of her neck. His movement dragged her dress along with him, and cool air swirled around her exposed stockings. Could their predicament worsen any further? Then the bench fell, and Darcy was crushed atop her again.

"I am not strong enough," cried Miss Darcy. "I will fetch help. The others must still be in the maze."

"Wait, Georgiana," Darcy began, but it was too late. Her footsteps were already disappearing around the corner.

He tried to wrest free of the contraption once more before stopping to lift his head and peer down at Elizabeth. "Well, Miss Bennet, it seems we are destined to expose ourselves to all our relations."

"Hopefully only to those with discretion."

"Even so," he said, resuming his serious aspect, "you do realize the most likely outcome—"

"—will be we are obliged to marry." From the moment he confessed his feelings were unchanged and the rotten wood buckled beneath them, the idea was never far from her thoughts. "I know."

"Miss Bennet, I"—he swallowed and his stomach tensed—"I would not see you forced into a marriage you do not desire or wed to a man you do not like. I cannot guarantee matrimony will not be the inevitable result, but I assure you that I will make every effort to achieve an alternative—"

"Mr. Darcy." She uttered his name softly, imbuing it with all the tenderness she had secretly harbored toward him. How touching that even in this difficulty he was considering her first.

"—and if I cannot, you have my solemn promise that I will do everything in my power—"

"Mr. Darcy." She tried again with more insistence.

"—to ensure your happiness and—"

"Fitzwilliam."

He ceased speaking and stared at her.

"I will marry you."

He blinked twice in succession. His lips parted a fraction.

She smiled. "If you had asked, I would have said yes."

"Are you certain the circumstances have not compelled you to such an exigency?"

"Before this worthless bench collapsed, I was about to answer that my feelings are quite opposite to what they were in the spring, that I am ashamed they were ever other than what they are now, and that it has been many months since my sentiments have been in harmony with yours." If only she could touch his face and wipe away the moisture gathering in the corners of his eyes, but her arms were pinned to her sides. "If we must blame the bench for anything, I think it is only for hastening the inevitable."

"Then God bless this bench."

She chuckled and went silent. If he beheld her with affection and longing before, it was nothing to the way he regarded her now. Something new and warm, tremulous and startling, kindled within her.

"If our circumstances were anything than what they presently are," he said, his tone low, "I would kiss you."

She searched his face. How rapidly the alien and unfamiliar dissipated. Now every line and whisker, the dense brows and thick lashes, the Cupid's bow above his lip were an invitation to be known and loved.

Heat rose in her cheeks. "I would not object."

His pulse accelerated, throbbing through his coat and her pelisse. His breath was warm on her face, murmuring his love and her name. Never had those letters been united with such allure. Her every sense was poised—

"Lizzy!" A voice shouted, succeeded immediately by footsteps trampling the gravel walk.

Elizabeth's body jerked, and Darcy pushed away as far as he could. She twisted her head, trying to see who approached, and winced at the forgotten ache in her back. Jane was flying toward them with Miss Darcy on her heels and several others following.

"Mr. Darcy!" Jane exclaimed.

Darcy muttered something unintelligible.

Elizabeth tried to call out that she was well, but a series of coughs drowned her attempt.

The confusion of exclamations and movement jostled and pushed them but did nothing to bring freedom. Not until Darcy bellowed for a halt and directed their sisters in an organized approach was any progress made. The entire process seemed muddled and slow, but Elizabeth was grateful when the pressure eased. Darcy crawled out and turned to brace his shoulder against the buckled frame. He pried her from her prone position and lifted her to her feet.

Her sisters crowded around, their hands brushing at her back and their voices garbled with concern. Jane's lovely face shimmered in waves. Elizabeth pressed her palms to her eyes. When she removed them, Jane's features blurred into a halo of light. Elizabeth squinted at Mary and Kitty, who were peering back at her with odd attention. A cloud of radiant pinpricks in their hair made it difficult to see. She tried to turn and find Darcy, but her neck was stiff and then her feet would not obey, her legs twisted, and she was falling, falling, her heart careening. Darkness descended over all.

*****

"Lizzy."

Cool air fanned her face.

"Lizzy, wake up. It is time to depart."

Elizabeth opened her eyes. She still sat in the pew where she had fallen asleep on first entering the sanctuary. Jane sat beside her, an open fan in her lap. Mary held her hand on the other side, and Kitty knelt in the pew ahead, her chin cushioned on fingers curled around the backrest's lip.

Elizabeth lifted her gaze to the high windows, dust motes swirled, and she remembered. She was praying for Darcy and giving thanks for the previous twelvemonth when she fell asleep. It was all a figment of her slumbering imagination: the rotten bench, their indelicate situation, her assent to a proposal he never made. Even Mr. Darcy himself. She sighed. What she would not give to be in her own bed that she might burrow her face into her pillow and resume where the dream left off or, barring that, indulge in a good cry. It was all so real.

She turned to Jane. "Were you able to find what you needed?"

Jane's brows knit.

"To finish your shopping?" clarified Elizabeth.

Jane glanced at Mary and Kitty before smiling her gentle smile. "We did, and it is kind of you to enquire, but at present I am only concerned for your welfare."

"Whatever for?" Elizabeth forced a brightness she did not feel. "I may have been more tired than I acknowledged and rested longer than planned, but there is no cause for worry."

Mary addressed Jane. "She must have struck her head with greater force than we realized."

"Struck my head?" Elizabeth probed her crown, but pain only radiated from the center of her back.

"You fainted in the garden," Jane said, "and Mr. Darcy carried you into the church. Do you not recall it?"

"Mr. Darcy is here?" Elizabeth straightened to search for him, and sparks danced in her vision. She subsided with equal rapidity. Was it possible she had not been dreaming after all?

"He has only gone to call for the carriages and will return directly."

Kitty snickered. "You should be glad you cannot remember, for we found you in the most compromising position. Your gown was nearly to your knees, and Mr. Darcy was—"

"Kitty, hush." Jane remonstrated. "Do not be distressed, Lizzy. Mr. Darcy explained everything."

"He did?" What precisely did he explain? Elizabeth pressed one hand to her cheek. Heat burned through her glove. "Please tell me what happened."

"He said the wood was deteriorated, and the bench you were seated on gave way beneath your combined weight. Apparently, you were trapped for some time, but it was clearly an accident. We all know he is too much of a gentleman to ever impose on you."

Another gurgle of laughter erupted from Kitty. This was confirmation enough.

"Then we must marry," Elizabeth blurted.

Her sisters exchanged a knowing look, as if she had spoken nonsense or they had information of which she was ignorant.

"No," Jane said, addressing her with the patient tone she reserved for their little Gardiner cousins, "no, while I am certain that Mr. Darcy is prepared to do what is right, considering there was no public spectacle, I do not see that such an extremity will be necessary."

Panic welled in Elizabeth. Though the bench actually had collapsed, perhaps she struck her head and only imagined the conversation with Darcy. "But, but—"

"Please do not fret." Mary squeezed her hand. "It is no surprise that you are confused, for you were nearly insensible by the time we arrived. I only hope you will forgive me for being so selfish. If I had accompanied you, this might have been avoided."

"Of course I forgive you," Elizabeth squeezed her hand in return, "but I do not see that your presence would have made any difference."

Kitty chortled. "The only difference would have been Lizzy and Mary under the bench and Mr. Darcy to rescue them."

A throat cleared, low and masculine. They all jumped.

Darcy stood in the aisle, immaculate and unruffled, with no trace of having spent a portion of his afternoon pinned with her beneath a garden bench. "Miss Elizabeth, I trust you are feeling improved?"

Such formality. How was she to respond after all that passed between them, if indeed it occurred? "Yes, sir, and I understand I have you to thank for my rescue."

His color might have deepened, but he only inclined his head and turned his attention to Jane, who rose from the pew.

"Miss Bennet," he said, "your transportation awaits, though I hope you will not mind I took some liberties with the seating. If you would accompany Miss

Elizabeth in my carriage, I thought she might be easier as it is more commodious. My sister and her companion shall ride with Miss Mary and Miss Kitty in the Gardiner's coach. Is that amenable?"

Jane agreed.

A brief shuffle ensued as her sisters gathered their articles and prepared to depart. No sooner did Elizabeth gain her feet and achieve the aisle than she was overshadowed by Darcy, who stepped near enough that she could identify his now familiar scent.

"Miss Elizabeth, if you will allow me, may I have permission to carry you?"

"Thank you," she said, "but that will not be necessary."

"Please"—his intense dark eyes entreated her—"you have already been injured twice while in my care."

"I hardly think you can take credit for a decaying bench."

"But it was my weight—"

"And how were you to guess I would lose consciousness?"

"I should have known better than to stand you on your feet so abruptly." His earnestness chiseled away at her uncertainty.

"If you will lend me your arm, Mr. Darcy, I think that will be more than adequate."

He obliged with celerity. Elizabeth's sisters preceded them out the door and started down the granite steps with a haste unfettered by the fatigue of illness or injury.

Elizabeth paused on the stoop, the wind whistling in her ears, while Darcy latched the door. His carriage stood mere yards away, though it may as well have been a mile. She leaned into him without thinking. Before she could object, he swept her into his arms and cradled her against his chest.

"Mr. Darcy!" she protested. She appraised his handsome features, so near once again—a regal brow above intelligent eyes and a firm mouth that communicated sincerity and kindness when he smiled. Such as he was bestowing on her now.

"I admire your resilience," he said, "but there is no virtue in being stubborn, particularly when your strength is spent."

He was correct, though she did not admit it aloud and only rested her cheek against his shoulder. He moved down the steps with telling caution. Bewilderment still clouded her mind and made her thoughts sluggish. Their forced intimacy that seemed so real when she first awoke had taken on increasingly dream-like properties. Did she really confess her admiration? His every look and word, the very manner in which he was holding her seemed an affirmation, but she would not be able to rest until she was certain.

"What happened with the bench," she began.

"We need not speak of it now."

"But what I said to you—"

"Neither need you feel bound by what was exchanged between us." His brow furrowed. "Our sisters all agreed to the prudence of discretion."

Jane turned aside to the Gardiner's coach for a moment, and they were nearly at Darcy's carriage.

"Please. You must allow me to finish. Mary said I was insensible, but I remember what I said to you." Elizabeth's voice caught, and she swallowed back the rising emotion. "I recall every word, but what I need to know is"—she looked up at him as he set her on her feet to hand her through the open door—"was I only dreaming?"

She thought he whispered her name as she stepped into a spacious cabin fitted up with more elegance than she had ever seen in a conveyance. The carriage dipped sideways with Darcy's weight. He directed her to the forward facing bench and perched on its edge beside her.

"Elizabeth," he said, clasping her hand in his own. "If you were dreaming, then so was I."

His cravat rose and fell with his chest, one hand slid to grip her shoulder, and the other tipped her chin. His lips were warm and soft on hers, his touch gentle and brief, and the assurance of his love streamed into her very soul.

When she opened her eyes, Jane stood at the carriage door, shock evident on her face. How was it they escaped the garden episode unscathed only to be caught now? Darcy must have read her mirroring expression, for he swiveled about.

.

"Please allow me, Miss Bennet." He shifted to assist Jane onto the bench beside Elizabeth.

"Lizzy…" Jane murmured in soft reproach, her cheeks pink and eyes round.

Elizabeth sensed Darcy's attention on her and rotated to meet his gaze. A slow smile tugged at one corner of his mouth and spread across his face with an infectious light.

"If you cannot laugh in moments like these," he said, "then what can you do?"

# FINALE

*January 1813, Meryton, Hertfordshire*

Elizabeth squinted against the refracted brilliance as they exited Meryton's church to the ovation of well-wishers and a dusting of snow. The newly minted Mr. and Mrs. Bingley preceded them toward Darcy's carriage, which was waiting to transport the wedding party to Longbourn for a celebratory breakfast.

Just over three weeks had passed since her preposterous reunion with Darcy: a whirlwind of dressmakers, dinners, and wedding preparations. She could not spend as much time with him as she would have wished, but they enjoyed enough conversation to bespeak a glowing future, like touring a home by candlelight and glimpsing the comforts and glories morning would reveal. How could she enter into this new year with any but the highest expectations? Elizabeth tilted her head to meet his eyes trained on her.

"May I ask why you are smiling at me so broadly?" he said and smiled in response.

"Are you happy?"

"To the depths of my being." He pressed her arm within his, but then his smile dimmed. "No, that is not entirely accurate. What I feel surpasses happiness—I know joy, Elizabeth."

She searched his face and found the truth of his words written in each contour. Any confession seemed inadequate to what she felt, such a tumult of joy and love, hope and desire, and beneath that something stronger still, riven with the force of gratitude that went beyond themselves.

But she could not speak of that now and only said, "As do I."

Several strides brought them to the carriage, revealing Jane and Bingley already installed on the rearward bench and too captivated by one another to heed their companions. Elizabeth gathered her skirts, preparing for Darcy to hand her in, but he bent his head beside hers.

"Oh, and Mrs. Darcy"—his low voice brushed across the bare skin above her collar, causing the fine hairs at her nape to rise and sending a shiver through her—"the bed is mine."

# GOLD, ALL GOLD

*November 1811, Hertfordshire*

Miss Elizabeth Bennet grunted and pulled with all her strength, but an earthen maw had swallowed her ankle and locked its jaw. Tangled branches from the fallen tree masked the offending hole and grated against her calf like sharpened teeth.

Thank heavens her mother was not present to hear her utter such unfeminine and inelegant noises! She paused to catch her breath and could not resist a grin. Then again, there would be time enough to indulge the comedic element in her predicament once she was free. She pulled her leg, redoubling her labors—and her grunting.

It was no use. Elizabeth exhaled, breath visible in the foggy autumn morning. Her bonnet rested to one side where she placed it when she grew overheated from her efforts at escape. She peered through the dimness to scan the Netherfield woods. Ashen trunks soared skyward from the carpet of crumbling leaves, the filmy fretwork of mist clinging to their skeletal branches overhead.

She stripped off her gloves and scooted across the ground closer to her ensnared foot. If she could reach to untie the laces, she might be able to wriggle out of her walking boot. Her ankle ached, but she ignored the discomfort. Liberating herself was more urgent. How she would return to the house was of secondary import.

Dead leaves crunched, and her head jerked toward the sound. Something was coming. Though the local woods were not known to harbor predators, her imprisoned leg made her position vulnerable. There. A shadow slipped from tree to tree. Her heart rate increased.

He emerged into her sight, his greatcoat settling around his legs in a black swirl. She swallowed a groan. What perversity drove Mr. Darcy into the grove this early that he of all people should find her? Thus far in her sojourn at Netherfield, he had amused himself with either staring or making enigmatic remarks, such as his inexplicable proposal to dance a reel.

"Miss Bennet, are you hurt?" Several swift strides brought him to crouch beside her, concern in his eyes. At least he was not unfeeling.

She forced a light laugh. "Only stuck, I think."

"Allow me to assist you." He leaned over to examine her foot where it was wedged beneath the toppled tree.

"You are some distance from the trail. May I enquire as to your object?"

"I wished to see the sun rise above the fog. This is the quickest route to Miller's Hill, but I slipped when I was climbing over the trunk."

"Most young ladies would have skirted such an impediment."

How like him to reprove her at such a moment. She lifted her chin. "Most young ladies would not be walking before breakfast, nor would they stray from the path." Was that a fleeting smile as he looked down? Surely not. Her brows drew together.

"May I have permission to attempt to extract your foot?"

"Of course."

He worked for several minutes, bending and breaking small branches to afford better access. Then his hands wrapped about her lower leg, and he began manipulating it. She stared off into the fog-shrouded trees, biting her lip against the pain. Perhaps she sustained greater injury than she first assumed.

When he released her, she dropped her gaze from the woods. He was removing his gloves, probably having arrived at the same conclusion as she when he stumbled upon her. He knelt in the dirt and bent close to the trunk, his fingers at work on her laces. His coat pooled behind him in a black waterfall. At least she wore long, thick stockings that would prevent unwelcome contact with his skin. She did not cherish any desire to know what that might reveal.

He tugged on her leg.

She whimpered but managed not to cry out.

His sharp gaze sought hers. "You are hurt."

"My ankle. I think it may have twisted."

He rocked back on his heels and into a squat. "If I roll the tree a little, do you think you could remove your foot?"

The good-sized beech was recently fallen, probably in the storm that caught Jane a few days prior. Darcy was built on a formidable scale, tall and broad of back and shoulder. Still. "Even you could not—"

He glowered and she ceased mid-statement, irritated but not wanting to insult her erstwhile rescuer.

"On three." He surveyed the log, selected two sturdy branches for greatest leverage, braced his shoulder against the mottled bark, and began to count. His face reddened, the cords of his neck straining against his cravat. With a creak, the pressure eased. She yanked free, groaning as she withdrew her throbbing limb.

He returned to kneel before her. "May I?"

"Thank you." She swiped at her face, embarrassed by her tears.

He pushed her skirts aside and removed her shoe. His fingers probed the injury with astonishing gentleness. The sprain was tender but not excruciating.

"There are no rents in your stocking, and I cannot feel that it is broken. You are very fortunate, Miss

Bennet." He tied her boot without haste, rose, and extended his hand. "Do you think you can stand?"

Her ungloved fingers closed around his naked wrist even as his did around hers. She sucked in a breath. Dizziness seized her, yet without even a hint of nausea.

\*\*\*\*\*

Elizabeth awakened in an amber world, unexpectedly familiar though she could not account for why. A gilded haze stretched as far as the eye could see. There were no trees, only limitless fields of gold, their flaxen stalks rolling in an imperceptible wind. Before her stretched a sea, if sea it could be called, all gold, pure gold, as still and glassy as a mirror. The sun, an enormous glowing orb somehow muted in the gold of that place, hovered over the horizon. She stretched her bare arms before her, as bronze and smooth as a sculpture. She reached with one marveling hand to feel her own skin, surprised that it was warm flesh.

Bronze fingers larger than her own trailed down her arm to grasp her hand. The sensation would have raised gooseflesh in her waking reality, but she only stared as the shiny track left by his touch faded. How was it possible that she was here with him?

Darcy moved before her. She lifted her eyes to his face, the strong angles of cheek and brow and jaw highlighted in the tawny light. His dark hair was gilt-tipped, and a sun blazed in his irises. She had always considered him handsome, regardless of his manners, but in this place he was magnificent. He was staring at her in his customary fashion. Except this time with admiration—perhaps even awe.

"You—" His other hand caressed her cheek.

She could not move, could hardly breathe in the dense, balmy air.

"Come." His hand closed tighter about hers, and he led them into the liquid gold.

She did not hesitate, although she felt she ought to have resisted. They were both fully dressed. Darcy still wore his greatcoat, but she could not say where her pelisse had disappeared nor how she came to be clothed in such an exquisite ball gown with its sweeping décolletage and caramel embroidery drizzled in a confection of curlicues. The fabric swirled and flowed about her in an endless variation of spun gold. The gown was more elegant than any she had worn or owned, indeed, more elegant than any fashion plate she had seen.

The sea rose thick and warm around her calves and knees and thighs. Wading proved difficult, but Darcy propelled them implacably forward, as if leading into the heart of the sun which seemed to grow and expand to monumental proportions.

Elizabeth passed a palm across the concentric rings created by their passage and checked over her shoulder. Wavelets lapped at the shore with a metallic glint, already many yards behind them.

When the liquid closed over her exposed shoulders, she balked. Darcy stopped, the shimmering expanse reaching only to his chest. His coat floated behind him in a wake of deepest bronze. He arched a brow, urging her onward.

"I am afraid that I am out of my depth, sir."

He smiled—such a smile as she had never seen. Then he sank almost beneath the surface. His arms connected with her submerged body, and she gasped. He straightened, lifting and cradling her against him. She did not protest, did not want to protest. He strode further into the golden deep. She looped her arms around his shoulders, oddly riveted by the gold dripping like honey from her bronze skin and coursing slowly down his coat. His chest rose and fell against her, and the motionless sun chiseled his noble profile into resplendence.

"Oh, Elizabeth." His voice was full of mystery and gravitas and near, so very near—

\*\*\*\*\*

With a shock, the golden light succumbed to shadow and the clement air grew cold. She floundered for awareness, caught fleetingly between two worlds, and found herself standing in the veiled, leaden woods.

Mr. Darcy's hands were shaking her shoulders gently. "Miss Elizabeth."

She shivered.

"Are you well?" Proximity magnified his concern. "You seemed faint. I thought you might—"

She writhed in the grip of conflicting emotions, still dazed and sated from being in his arms. She stared into his inscrutable eyes, searching for recognition. Was that fire dwindling in their inky depths? It could not be. He could not be...

Apprehension clawed at her. When seized by such an impression, she was unconscious of what occurred around her. Her family said the vision passed in a twinkling, though her countenance usually reflected some sentiment—peace or delight, anger or disdain. No one was privy to what she saw.

He stepped back a full pace. "Are you certain that you are well?"

"Yes, quite," she placed tentative weight on her sore ankle and winced, "though I may require your arm to hobble back to Netherfield."

"Of course." But he did not move to assist her. His eyes narrowed, alert with curiosity and something else. He was troubled.

Prudence necessitated she resolve it now, while it was still fresh in his memory and where they could not be overheard. "What did you see, Mr. Darcy?"

He started. "See?"

"Yes, when you took my hand to help me up."

He spread his fingers and turned his hand to examine both sides as if the appendage did not belong to him. "I cannot—"

She sighed. "I will know the best manner in which to explain if you will kindly tell me what you saw." What emotion might he have read in her face while she was lost to a vision of reveling in his embrace? It was exceedingly awkward. She needed his account that she might not reveal more than necessary, only enough to reassure him and secure his silence. And there was that sliver of hope she dare not entertain.

"You—I saw—" He struggled through some inner dilemma. "There was a flash and the woods seemed afire, and then the very air was rippling with gold and you were—" The words tumbled out of him, one hastening upon another. His face contorted. "I am blathering like an idiot. This is ludicrous."

She did not move to touch him, but her heart thudded in incredulity and anticipation. "Go on. I was?"

He looked away. "It is not worthy of conversation. Let us return."

"No," she cried. She must not forego this opportunity. "Please. It was not your imagination. I mean, it was in your imagination, but it was—oh, why can I not be coherent?" She wrung her hands, staring at him and wrestling with indecision. "I could show you what you saw, if you wish."

His brows drew together. "What do you mean?"

She took one step, closing the distance between them by a third. "I must touch your face."

His mouth flattened into a line, but his lengthier stride brought him within reach. "This is utter madness."

She stretched her fingers upward, anxiety coiling in her stomach. She had never admitted this much, never done this outside her family. Never. What if it should prove to be him? She must make certain, one way or the other. Two fingertips connected with his temple.

*****

Immediately, Elizabeth was transported into Darcy's arms, this time without dizziness. It was not at all what she expected. Her mind whirled with the implications, yet she could not be troubled to puzzle it out, not here. They stood in the golden sea, under the ardor of an amber sun. She removed her hand from his face. His head swiveled systematically, taking in his exotic domain.

He appraised her nestled in his arms and blinked twice. Light glinted from the tips of his lashes, and the fire rekindled in his eyes. "What is this place?"

"It is not so easily defined." She smiled, trying to put him at ease. "It is a product of your mind and dreams, your heart and character."

"I should recall if I dreamed all in gold."

"Not like that, more emblematic. What does gold connote to you?"

"Wealth, certainly, but I am not one to dwell on my own consequence." His affronted scowl almost made her laugh.

"Gold might imply something you value highly, something precious." She looked about again. "This realm, do you not feel it? There is a purity, a warmth to it."

One corner of his mouth tipped up at some unvoiced thought. The quiet stretched. He grew solemn again.

"You are here." He bent his forehead against hers, and heat flooded her. "Like some bronze sculpture breathed to life."

"So are you."

He raised his head. She followed his gaze to the immense sun where it hung suspended, its amber light gleaming in a straight swathe down the brass sheet, a lustrous path beckoning them.

"Where are we going?" he asked.

"Into the sun it would seem," she dragged a finger through the tepid brink, "but I know not. You are the one who led us here."

"I simply strolled into the sea and presumed to carry you without so much as a by-your-leave."

"If you let go, I would drown."

"Then I will never let go." His voice resonated with conviction and tenderness.

She pillowed her head on his shoulder, comfortable, content, unconcerned. How long had she yearned and waited for one to whom her gift would not be a burden and despaired that she should ever know the consolation of being loved and held? She could linger forever in the intimacy of his gilded embrace.

*****

Something scratchy beneath her cheek dissolved Elizabeth's contemplations. She lifted her head from its cushion against the black wool of Darcy's greatcoat and found she was once again in the cloaked woods. Heat rose in her cheeks as she pulled away.

He released her.

"Forgive me, Mr. Darcy, for imposing myself on you."

"I believe it to be quite the reverse. For it appears I have been entertaining you in my dreams." His cheeks were ruddy, though whether from the frosty air or from embarrassment she could not determine. "It seems my secret has been exposed."

"As has mine," she said. Naturally he preferred her ignorance, which meant she must find some means to bear the deprivation. She folded her hands. "You may depend on my discretion as I will depend on yours. Now that you are assured you are not going mad, we may forget the whole."

"I am assured of no such thing, but I cannot forget. I meant what I said."

She held her breath.

"I will never let you go, not unless you ask it of me."

How could she reconcile the luster of those golden moments with the aloof, imposing gentleman who had scorned her? Was she really so faulty in her judgments?

In the prolonged quiet, he turned to retrieve their personal articles from the ground. He passed her the bonnet and then her gloves. She pulled them on. Buttery soft leather encased her fingers, and she brushed at the dirt that marred their mustard yellow nap. He donned his as well and offered his arm.

Never had a vision led her astray, and generosity and integrity epitomized her underlying impression. There was only one choice, even if he was the imperious Mr. Darcy.

She bestowed an unmistakable smile of assent on him and decisively accepted his elbow. "Where shall you lead us now?"

An answering smile illumined his countenance. "Where is this Miller's Hill of which you spoke?"

"Not far," she gestured behind them, "at the top of the rise I was attempting. The trail offers a less abrupt route, though it is also more circuitous. But I do not think I could manage either hill or trail at present."

"I would not ask it, but I should still like to view the sun cresting the fog. With you."

"Perhaps we might happen upon one another again some morning, once my leg is healed."

He bent down, his arms came behind her shoulders and knees, and she was swept off her feet.

"I suggest we go now," he said.

"You cannot seriously intend to carry me up the entire hill."

"I will own you are not quite as weightless as you were in the sea, but I am equal to it if you will guide me along the most direct path."

She laughed but gave him instruction, and he began their steady ascent through the trees. The crisp leaves rustled and twigs occasionally snapped beneath his boots.

"Tell me more about this extraordinary talent you possess."

She regarded him with wonder. "You think it an advantage?"

"Of course. To be able to sketch another's character without error, who would not want such ability?"

"Do not be misled. I err as often as anyone." Her laugh was soft. "It is as much burden as blessing. When I was haunted by nightmares as a child and Papa was at a loss for what to do, he took me to the rector."

"Did that help?"

"He called it a gift of discernment, and in time I learned to use it wisely." She shook her head. "The darkness, the brokenness that hides in the human soul— it is more than I can bear. For that reason, as well as my intention to avoid what is in essence a forced confidence, I eschew contact with exposed skin."

"And if you do not, as when you took my hand, then what happens?" He glanced at her.

She ceased mapping the shadow of dark whiskers along her jaw, and warmth climbed her neck. She tried to answer as if he had not interrupted her scrutiny. "Every person is unique. Fragmentary images rush into my mind and convey an impression of that person's character and desires. My father, for example, his sphere is a contemplative one, all browns—leather and coffee and books.

"And my sister Jane, hers is a flower garden in softest shades of serenity and sweetness. Sometimes I ask her to allow me a peek just for its soothing effect." She smiled in remembrance but did not mention how often of late she observed Bingley ambling about in the peaceful rosiness of Jane's thoughts.

Darcy's brow furrowed. "But they are unaware of what you see?"

"They know nothing, experience nothing, not unless I show them."

Perspiration began to bead across his upper lip. "And your capacity to share these images, how does that operate?"

"I could count on one hand the times I have done it. My father and sisters find the dizziness and nausea disconcerting." She angled her head. "Did you?"

"Not at all. I experienced no discomfort."

His answer surprised her, but she chose to continue her explanation. "Generally, with two fingers to the temple I can communicate the whole, and the person watches over my shoulder as it were."

"It is always exact, the precise vision that you saw initially?"

Elizabeth nodded and he frowned.

They exited the wood and the fog in the same moment, as if the mist were cotton batting stuck fast in the branches and restrained from evaporating into the blue sky. Darcy labored from the exertion, his breathing deep and the muscles in his arms shifting beneath her back and legs as she swayed against him. A few last surging strides brought them to the summit. He set her down in the crown of greying grass.

The sun hovered well above the horizon, its blinding radiance amplified by boundless white. The fog stretched into the distance, hiding the landscape beneath a fluffy down coverlet. It undulated leisurely, breaking here and there around pointed treetops and solitary hills. Though sound was muffled, the air was fresh and calm.

"You have led me to a golden world and now one blindingly silver." Darcy paused in his unhurried revolution to smile down at her. "What shall I expect next?"

"Is it not glorious?"

"You will love the peaks of Derbyshire." His eyes never left her face. "Miss Elizabeth, if no one can see your vision unless you share it, why did I catch a glimpse before you showed me?"

His repeated use of her Christian name registered, but she did not comment and only scanned the skyline. "As it has never before happened, I could not say," she looked back to him, "though I will own that I am interested in what you observed."

"It was just a glimpse, the briefest moment, and what I saw was you. You were stunning, standing on the shore of that golden sea in a—well, a gown unlike any I have seen."

"I have never before been drawn into another's vision." She did not mention that his inspiration conjured her dress.

"Have you not?"

"Oh no, Mr. Darcy," she pressed his sleeve, "I am not explaining this well at all. Today was the first time, the only time, that I have been a participant. Always I am an observer. I merely watch, as through a window—which is why you are unique. Not only was I present, but you knew me."

"And the second time, what you showed me," he squinted into the brilliance, "it was not a repetition of that initial glimpse I received."

"With you, it is different. With you"—she swallowed—"when I touched you, what was past vanished and the vision resumed in unbroken sequence. We share that memory and the making of it."

"Elizabeth." He drew closer and squeezed her upper arm with one hand. "How dearly I should like to step into your dreams."

Was that why she recognized the familiarity of the amber hue? The same glow illuminated those passing moments when she fell into sleep and first woke, and shielded recollection of her dreams in impenetrable light.

She studied him in astonishment. "I think you have."

"If these visions require an intimate connection," he nudged her bonnet back on her head, "what would transpire if I kiss you?"

She knew not, but something sputtered and ignited deep within.

He peeled one yellow glove from her hand, meticulous in his deliberateness, and pocketed it in his greatcoat. He raised her bare fingers in his gloved ones and held them slightly away from his temple. "Allow me to share your dreams."

His head drew near, and his other hand found her nape. He pressed her fingers to his face. For a transitory moment, his cheek felt cool beneath her palm and his lips warm and soft upon her own. Then gold exploded in her senses.

\*\*\*\*\*

They were wrapped in the sun-drenched sea, rocked in the buoyant waters. The ochre sky descended around them, a million tiny sparks flickering down, fiery flecks floating on molten gold. They caught in Darcy's hair, on his brows and lashes, on his cheeks and nose. Elizabeth brushed a cloud from the shoulder of his coat. He laughed with her, its timbre cascading with humor and joy.

He took her in his solid arms and kissed her until in that glittering, gleaming realm where gold ran to gold her awareness was consumed by only him.

*****

Then everything faded—the gilded world, the hilltop view, the misty woods.

Elizabeth's eyelids rose reluctantly to the yellow and orange flames curling from the coals. Where was she? Her gaze flitted from wall to wall like a moth caught in a glass. She sat on the sofa in Netherfield's drawing room, the gloom broken only by the dying blaze and a single candle on a small round table. But for the fire's sighing, all was silent and still.

The day scrolled before her memory: a sunny morning walk alone; her mother's mortifying call; hours at Jane's bedside; a visit to the library; another stroll out of doors before dinner; the evening in company with the Bingleys, Hursts, and Darcy; and none of the bizarre occurrences her sleep fabricated. The others must have retired and left her to doze. Betrayal that she was forsaken and relief that she was alone warred for ascendancy. Jane would be missing her.

She started to leave but sank back, overcome again with the strangeness of her dreams, with their intensity—and that she should dream of such intimacies with Mr. Darcy, toward whom she did not nurture a single tender feeling. She touched timid fingers to her lips.

Hinges complained. The door swung inward to admit a towering figure.

She gaped at him.

Darcy placed his candle beside its mate on the small table and strode to her, glancing once over his shoulder. "It is very late. I thought you would have returned to your chambers by now."

"No, I—"

"My apologies that you were abandoned, but I insisted you not be disturbed. I am afraid your ministrations to your sister have been overtaxing."

Elizabeth did not know what to say, what was real and what imagined. His very presence unnerved her, sent every sense reeling.

"Come, madam, rouse yourself." His voice was commanding. "You must not linger here all night."

She permitted him to pull her to her feet and stepped gingerly on her injured leg. There was no pain. Her ankle remained as sound as it had ever been.

Darcy led her toward the exit and paused at the table but did not move to give her a candle. He bowed his head. She studied the breadth of his back, the same back that rounded over her boots, lifted a tree, and carried her. She could not rid her mind of the images. She would never view him in the same manner again.

He turned with unexpected swiftness, and his hands enveloped hers. "I must bid you good night here."

She was startled but did not withdraw from his grasp. Soil underlined the half-moon of his thumbnail.

He upturned one of her hands, rummaged in his coat pocket, and pressed a single mustard yellow glove into her palm.

She stared, uncomprehending. Did she not give both gloves to a servant when she returned that afternoon? She examined it. Dirt smudged several fingertips. "Where?"

"You must have forgotten it on your walk."

Her fingers closed around the supple leather involuntarily. "I do not understand."

"I think you do." He leaned down, his voice mellifluent in her ear. "Your dreams are as beautiful as you are, Elizabeth, and I should like nothing more than to bring them to fruition."

Darcy straightened and beheld her with meaningful eloquence. How could he know? It was inconceivable. Every faculty deserted her.

His eyes held her immobile. His fingers met her temple, his stroke a fleeting fire.

She could not support herself and reached for him as the world melted into gold, all gold.

# EDEN UNASHAMED

## PART I

I am not a man of many words. I never have been. I would rather listen than speak, which is fortunate, for my closest friends, both Bingley and Colonel Fitzwilliam, boast a surfeit of speech. And my dearest, loveliest, most enchanting Elizabeth is rarely at a loss for words. This is but one among her many qualities that I appreciate and enjoy. As in the old proverb, 'a word fitly spoken is like apples of gold in frames of silver,' her uncanny discernment enables her to know exactly what to say in a given situation—at least, in situations not involving me, but that is another story.

I have repeatedly witnessed her exercise this ability. In short, she makes each person with whom she speaks feel as if he or she is the center of the world, genuinely and sincerely. Therefore, everyone loves to speak with her. Nor is this an affectation as it is with many ladies of my sphere, who merely wish to display their facility for conversation.

Lately, Elizabeth has been wielding this formidable skill in praise of my person. I will not deny that I find it gratifying—supremely gratifying, in fact—to be told frequently and fervently not only that I am loved, admired and respected, but also precisely why. And that is what brought me to this juncture. Although I converse with her more easily than with anyone else, even my darling sister Georgiana, I still find it difficult to communicate my deepest sentiments. Elizabeth would say I express myself quite well, but then she is generous. I alone am aware how my words too often fall short. A man who felt less might say more.

Thus, while I do not fancy myself a poet, I did set about to arrange some verses for her, which might properly convey my love and longing on the cusp of our marriage. I found an unexpected pleasure in this endeavor and was inspired to compose not one but two poems. If they dwell disproportionately on her beauty, that is a lover's prerogative. Of her intelligence, wit, compassion, and numerous other intangible virtues, I do not hesitate to extol her nor she to deflect my compliments as is her wont.

One poem I have reserved for a propitious moment on our wedding day. The other I secreted within the book she has been reading each evening. I will confess succumbing to the decidedly romantic appeal of her withdrawing to her bedchamber to pore over my poem alone and ruminate on it through the night.

However, I erred gravely in this mode of delivery. I ought to have realized that mischief was afoot when she acknowledged ignorance of my offering during our stroll among the shrubbery this morning. But it seemed a simple matter to return to the sitting room and locate the verses within the correct volume.

*****

"Kitty!"

Was it possible her name could wear thin from overuse like the sole of a dancing slipper? Kitty offered her mother the ribbon she had been twining round and round her fingers.

"Not the grosgrain." Mrs. Bennet objected. "I want you in your best looks. How else do you expect to catch a husband? There will be single men of large fortune in attendance, I am sure, what with all Mr. Darcy's and Mr. Bingley's fine friends and family here for the weddings."

While her mother was speaking, she yanked the wrinkled length from Kitty's hands and deftly located a wide satin version in the same shade. This bordered on the miraculous, considering the table was littered with a colorful tangle of ribbons, a profusion of lace, and a hodgepodge of accoutrements from fruit to feathers to flowers.

"But, Mamma…" whined Kitty. Trimming bonnets with her sister had been ever so much more fun. Lydia had not ordered her about and always divulged savory morsels of gossip.

"No, I will not brook any complaints. My nerves will not stand it." Mrs. Bennet raised her chin primly and shook her head in defiance. "I have worked too hard to have one daughter married, and Jane and Elizabeth will follow within the fortnight. You and Mary are next, I am determined, and you will not thwart me."

At this expostulation, Kitty caught an alarmed glance from Mary, the only other occupant of the sitting room. She promptly rose and excused herself.

Mrs. Bennet wrapped the satin ribbon over the crown of the bonnet. Holding it with one hand on each side of the brim, she straightened her arms and twisted the bonnet first one way and then the other, examining it from each angle. "Yes, I think that will do very nicely." Her eyes roved the table for a moment. "Kitty, my sewing basket, please. We will just tack this down."

Kitty sighed and retrieved the basket from its usual post next to her mother's armchair. With Mary at her books, Kitty was left to occupy their mother. The presence of her eldest sisters to interrupt the incessant soliloquies would have made it more bearable, but the gentlemen had arrived before Mamma came down. Both seemed excessively desirous of a private audience with their intended and swept Jane and Elizabeth from the room to gad about the shrubbery.

Kitty longed for some excitement and was sure to find it, if only her parents would allow her to accept her newlywed sister's invitation. But her father became positively churlish if she dared to mention visiting Mrs. Lydia Wickham in Newcastle. Taking her place as the youngest in the household was not fulfilling Kitty's expectations.

She cleared a space on the table, lifted the basket lid, and began rummaging through the disarray. But what was this? Kitty withdrew and opened what appeared to be a folded blank paper. The half-sheet was extravagant when a quarter would have done for so few words. She started reading and gasped. A hand flew to her mouth, but her eyes flew even faster across the lines.

"Oh my," she tittered, "oh my!"

"What?" asked her mother, snatching the paper from her hands.

"I cannot imagine that it was for you to read," Kitty said.

"What can you mean? It was in my sewing basket. Of course it is for me." Mrs. Bennet extended the paper in the same manner as she had the bonnet and squinted. "My, but the hand is rather small. Fetch my spectacles, dear."

Kitty did so with reluctance and then attempted to read over her mother's shoulder while Mrs. Bennet adjusted the glasses on her nose.

"Oh, goodness," Mrs. Bennet said. "Oh, that sly man! Why…" She waved the paper to cool her cheeks, which were ruddy with a deepening flush. "Why, I cannot think when your father last left me a love note."

"Surely you do not think it is from father?" Kitty could not imagine her father having ever written love letters to her mother.

"Well, of course I do. Who else would it be from? Shame on you, to think some other man would be leaving me love notes in my basket." She waggled a finger.

"But the writing is not Papa's."

"That does not signify. He is so fond of a joke, I daresay he had someone copy it out for him. Lizzy might have done it. She is that clever with a pen, although I cannot quite approve, considering."

"Really, Mamma, do you not think it might be from either Mr. Bingley or Mr. Darcy?" Kitty would have read it again, if her mother were not brandishing it like an errant lace tucker.

"And why would either of them be leaving me verses in my basket? Sometimes I think your father is right. How can you be so silly?" She reread the poem, shifting about to keep it from Kitty's eyes, and pressed it to her bosom with one hand while fanning her face with the other. "Oh, oh, but my heart is all atremble. I am feeling quite dizzy. My salts, my salts, Kitty, in my reticule."

Kitty departed on the errand in resignation, rolling her eyes as she left the room. If her mother would wear a pocket or an apron as did Mary that she might have her books about her, then her mother might have her salts at hand whenever she wished, instead of inconveniencing daughters and servants.

Although, in this instance Kitty could hardly blame her mother for a nervous attack. The verses were rather… she searched for an accurate word and dissolved in giggles. Well, excessively romantic to be sure. The idea that her father, who preferred to tease and trifle with his wife, would have made the effort to compose them, let alone had the inclination, was not only incredible but vaguely repellent. This required another reading. Her heart accelerated in anticipation.

Kitty rushed back to the sitting room, but instead of finding her mother slouched in her chair as expected, Mrs. Bennet appeared frozen in mid-motion partway across the room. She looked very much as if she had been tip-toeing. Her expression of guilty stealth savored of Lydia, whenever Kitty had caught her sneaking into her sisters' rooms to borrow an item without permission.

"Mamma?"

Mrs. Bennet reanimated. In three strides, she halted before Kitty and snatched the vial from her hand. "What a good girl! Thank you, child. My, but that poem quite took my breath away." She heaved an affected sigh. "Now, shall we return to our work?"

"But where are the verses? I should like to read them again." Kitty adopted as petulant and persistent a tone as she was able, knowing how well it had worked for Lydia. "I really do not think they are from Papa."

But her mother only smiled a secret smile. "They are very fine verses, and I cannot fault you for wishing to admire them. But there are some things"—she gave another great sigh—"that are for a married woman and not her maiden daughter. I am sure you will have many pretty verses from your husband someday. But you will have no hope to marry at all unless we finish these bonnets."

"But Mamma—" Kitty moved to the table and commenced a search for the poem in her mother's sewing basket and amidst the scattered piles.

"You will not find it, so you may as well quit." Mrs. Bennet chortled. "I have hidden it in a very safe place."

Kitty glanced around at any number of nooks where such a paper might be safeguarded, and she resolved to ferret it out. She *must* read it again.

*****

Bingley employed his handkerchief to wipe residual moisture from the sunny bench. He then settled his beautiful bride-to-be before seating himself next to her. The morning was a fairytale, crisp and fresh, the rime sparkling on the leaves like myriad pinpricks of light and even the air breathing with the coo of doves.

Jane shivered a little despite her pelisse and gloves. Bingley scooted closer and wrapped an arm about her shoulders. She was especially quiet since his arrival and her cheeks especially pink. It was cliché, but they were as luscious as strawberries bathed in cream. He inhaled deeply, drinking in her presence, and his chest swelled with happiness. If he had known his verses would induce such loveliness, he would have made the effort much sooner.

"Sweetest," he entreated.

Jane twisted her head to meet his gaze, and his breath caught. Her eyes were luminous, the softest shade of brown, like the coat of a fawn sleeping in the shade. Her beauty was irresistible.

He rotated toward her and reached across with his far hand to stroke the back of two fingers along her cheek. "So smooth."

The blush climbed toward her temples. She caught his hand that was caressing her face and restrained it in her lap, her eyes affixed to it.

"Charles," she said without looking up, "I found your verses."

He beamed. "And?"

"I am," she stammered, "I do not have words fit to express what it means to me." When her eyes caught his, they were glistening. Then she leaned over and kissed him, much to his surprise and delight. They had shared other kisses that were more passionate, but this was the first time she initiated an act of affection. The tenderness of her touch coursed through him from tip to toe. She straightened and lifted her eyes to his again, her face radiant with rosiness.

He withdrew his fingers from her grasp to caress her cheek once more. "Do not be embarrassed, sweetest. I could want for no better expression of gratitude."

Her smile quavered.

Satisfaction made him expansive. "If I scout out more such verses, will you thank me so again?"

Her brow furrowed a fraction. "Scout for them? Did you not compose them yourself?"

"I am flattered that you would rate my poetic ability so highly, but no." He paused, slightly mystified. "I thought the verses fitting after our discussion of sonnets."

"Sonnets?" The furrow deepened. "I would not say they quite qualify as a sonnet."

He slid back and took both her hands in his. "If you wish to be exact, of course, it was not the sonnet in its entirety. I only copied the most pertinent lines—the ones that reminded me of you."

"Oh!" She blushed furiously.

"Sweetest, have I made you uncomfortable? Would it relieve you if I clarified why I chose them?"

She flashed panicked eyes at him and shook her head. "Oh, no—please—I could not."

Bingley fiddled with his hands in perplexity. That his verses both pleased and disconcerted her was clear, but his attempt to ease her only increased her apparent anxiety. He was casting about for a safer topic when apprehension niggled at his mind.

"Jane, I left you four lines from one of Shakespeare's sonnets, but I would never wish to unsettle you." He grimaced. "Can you tell me if that is what you found?"

"No." She reddened further, right to the tops of her ears, though it hardly seemed possible.

"Is that 'no' to the Bard or 'no' to telling me?"

When she finally met his eye, agitation twisted her features. "Oh, this is too terrible. Charles, whatever am I going to do?"

Her distress alarmed him. "About what? What is it?"

"The verses."

"Well, yes, the verses, but what about them?"

"I hid them in my mother's sewing basket."

"I cannot imagine that is too terrible."

"Not the sonnet, I never saw that, but the other."

"But what of the other, you still have not told me."

"They were…" She took a deep breath and swallowed hard. "They were very passionate. If you did not write them, then I think they must be from Mr. Darcy to Lizzy."

"What?"

"They were in his hand. I recognized it."

"And still you read them?" He tried not to sound accusatory. "You thought them from me?"

"I found them precisely where you told me." Her tone was defensive, and he regretted speaking with such warmth. She continued, "I thought that maybe since you are such good friends you asked him to copy them, as I know you do not hold the highest opinion of your own handwriting. Not that I have ever found it wanting."

Bingley searched her face. He would not add to her discomfort by asserting he would never ask another man, not even his closest friend, to undertake such a delicate task. "Are you quite certain that they belong to Darcy?"

"Yes." She nodded. "I have seen his handwriting before. His precision is distinctive."

Bingley rose with haste. "Then I must find him this moment."

She clutched at his arm, startling him with her strength.

He permitted himself to be drawn down to the bench.

"No, Charles, I beg you. I could not bear the mortification of Mr. Darcy knowing that I read them. Please. We must find some other way."

"I will not pretend you did not see Darcy's poem."

"I would not ask it of you. But could we not return the verses to their original hiding place and then all will be well?"

"Perhaps," he allowed. "Tell me precisely what happened."

"I came down before everyone else. I was reading them in mother's chair, and I was so transported"—she blushed again—"that I did not hear the door until it was opening, so I tucked them into the sewing basket at my feet. It was only Lizzy, but I do not think I aroused her suspicions." Her subterfuge surprised him, knowing how close the sisters were.

"But you did not wish to share them with Elizabeth?"

"No," Jane said, her voice halting. "They are so very intimate. I do not think I would be quite comfortable sharing them with anyone but my… husband."

"Very well." He nodded, beset by a sympathetic dread on behalf of his friend, and clapped a hand to each thigh. "Let us hasten to the house. While you remove the paper from the sewing basket and restore it to the book, I will play lookout and attempt to divert any unwanted attention. Hopefully, as you say, all shall be well. I will do everything in my power to protect your anonymity, but if Darcy asks me directly, I must speak the truth." He stood and reached to assist her.

"Thank you. I understand, and Charles,"—her smile was imploring as she accepted his hand—"I am all anticipation to read your verses."

*****

Mary sat before her desk, staring with unseeing eyes at the volume in front of her. On her way to her room, she had glanced out the breakfast room window and observed Lizzy on Mr. Darcy's arm. Not only were they presently strolling in the gardens alone, they had been seated altogether too near one another in the sitting room earlier that morning. Jane and Mr. Bingley were somewhere about the grounds as well but could hardly be considered proper chaperones. Nothing good would come of it.

Mary straightened against her chair back. Were she to have five daughters, she would raise them very differently and not overlook these little breaches of decorum. But having children required marriage, marriage required a husband, and husbands were made of men, that other half of the species she found incomprehensible.

This reminded Mary of the matchmaking element in her imminent elevation to the status of eldest sister. Occasionally, she dreamt what it must be like to receive the degree of attention showered on Jane, but if it meant her mother continually pushing her toward this or that gentleman, she would as well forego the honor. However, and this was some reassurance, it was clear her mother planned to direct her energies toward Kitty as the more promising prospect. By comparison, how little care was being invested in the selection of Mary's gown for her sisters' nuptials, not that it bothered her in the slightest.

If her mother could take credit for any of the three marriages, Jane's was the most likely, since Mamma contrived to leave her and Mr. Bingley unchaperoned on multiple occasions, but even that was debatable. All this fuss over a wedding, even a double ceremony, was quite baffling. Why Jane and Lizzy had stayed awake half the nights this week talking and giggling mystified her. They seemed much more rational creatures before their respective betrothals.

In truth, Mary was rather disappointed in Lizzy, whom she considered next to her in intelligence. Certainly she could never be prevailed on to marry as proud a man as Mr. Darcy, no matter how rich he was. She could not imagine he would make an agreeable companion, nor easily be molded into one.

On the other hand, there was much to be said for the practicality of such a suitor, and Mr. Darcy did not appear in any way undisciplined or irreligious. At least Lizzy was purchasing the security of her future. With her elder sisters so well settled, Mary would not be obliged to marry if she did not wish it. Becoming the learned and wise spinster aunt who haunted Pemberley's library did have a certain appeal. She grinned and returned her attention to her book.

\*\*\*\*\*

Bingley tripped along the gravel drive, nearly dragged by Jane's swift pace. He had never witnessed her move with such haste, not that she was without good reason. He sympathized with her desire to restore Darcy's poem to its original hiding place before the error was discovered.

They were approaching Longbourn's front entry when the crunch of footsteps caused them to whirl in unison.

Elizabeth and Darcy were bearing down on them with comparable alacrity. They appeared as much on a mission as he and Jane, although Darcy's aspect was solemn while Elizabeth's was cheery. But there was nothing unusual in that juxtaposition.

After the other couple entered the sitting room, Bingley stopped beside the door in consternation. Mrs. Bennet was already at the table with Kitty, the offending basket nestled amidst an abundance of frippery. Jane's eyes widened for a moment, but she took her courage in hand and forged ahead. This was going to be much more difficult than anticipated.

"Mamma," Jane called, advancing toward her. "I had not an idea you would be trimming bonnets so early. Will you show me your progress thus far?"

She halted near the table, and Mrs. Bennet was only too eager to oblige. The muscles in Bingley's back tightened with apprehension for his beloved.

Jane listened and nodded her head while lifting the basket lid with surreptitious nonchalance and peering inside. She frowned, peeked at her mother who was still discoursing on her latest creation, and reached in to rifle through the contents.

"Jane!" said Mrs. Bennet. "Are you attending at all? Why are you meddling with my basket? Your new one is ever so much finer. I cannot imagine anything to interest you here."

"Of course, Mamma," acceded Jane, "but here are some"—she withdrew her fist and opened her hand—"some buttons that might serve well as an accent."

"Buttons?" Her mother looked askance. "On a bonnet?"

Jane shrugged an apology.

Bingley stifled a smirk. His dear girl could not dissemble to save her life, but at least she sidetracked her mother. Jane flicked her eyes at him, the shake of her head almost imperceptible. No poem.

Bingley was so engrossed by the exchange at the table that he failed to observe Elizabeth and Darcy. He swiveled his head to find both relaxed in their preferred settee, Darcy wearing a smug expression and Elizabeth looking as spirited as she typically did.

Grateful their attention was otherwise occupied, Bingley moved to the bookshelf and retrieved the volume in which he had hidden his verses with care on the previous night. He flipped through it, but no stray papers materialized. He glanced over his shoulder at Darcy and Elizabeth. They were still immersed in conversation and not attending. He searched several more times before replacing the book and then caught Jane's eye, trying to communicate their dilemma without words. Both his poem and Darcy's were lost. Everything was going terribly awry.

Before Bingley could formulate a plan, the door opened to admit Mr. Bennet.

"Oh, Mr. Bennet," his wife cried and practically flew from her chair to rush toward him. "You clever man! What a good joke!"

Bingley, who was standing nearest to them, blinked twice in amazement. Mrs. Bennet was batting her eyelashes and winking! He turned aside in embarrassment, but not before glimpsing the absolute bewilderment that overspread Mr. Bennet's face as well as the astonishment of everyone else present.

"My dear Mrs. Bennet," he addressed his wife with a wry tone, "while it is true I take great delight in devising such schemes, you have quite successfully, and rather unexpectedly I might add, turned the tables on me. Pray, enlighten me as to the nature of this diversion."

Mrs. Bennet wrapped her arm through his, drew close to his shoulder, and patted his chest with one hand. "Oh, how droll you are, Mr. Bennet, to pretend not to know."

Had Mrs. Bennet discovered the verses? Bingley frowned in speculation. That was unlikely, for if she did, she would be unable to keep it to herself.

Mr. Bennet's astonishment only increased. "Indeed, madam, you have me at quite the disadvantage."

"What a tease you are, husband." She twittered, her eyes bright and sounding much like her younger daughters. She rose up on her toes and whispered into his ear.

Bingley started at the impropriety, but Mr. Bennet's eyes only grew round.

"In that case, my dear, I suggest we conclude this discussion above stairs."

And with neither by-your-leave nor word of explanation, Mr. Bennet escorted his wife through the door.

Silence reigned for a full minute, and Bingley surveyed the shocked room. Elizabeth looked chagrined, Darcy affronted, Jane ashamed, and Kitty—her snicker started quietly enough, but within moments she was giggling outright. Elizabeth was the next to laugh, then Jane succumbed and Bingley could not help himself. It was all so exceedingly odd. Only Darcy remained stoic, yet Bingley thought he could perceive a mirthful light flickering behind even those dark eyes.

The door burst open again, and the room fell into immediate silence.

Bingley feared the senior Bennets were returned, but it was only Mary, whose hands were occupied securing her apron behind her back.

"Whatever is so funny?" Mary scanned them each in turn.

As if on cue, everyone present erupted in laughter. Even Darcy.

# PART II

Hands on hips, Kitty rotated with slow purpose, her eyes ranging over the sitting room. Where would her mother have hidden those deliciously romantic verses? Both engaged couples had departed hours ago to make calls and undertake wedding-related errands. Normally, she and her mother would have been thrilled to accompany them, but after her bizarre behavior, Mamma was oddly nowhere to be found.

Mary ate cold luncheon with her, but her atypical insistence on keeping Kitty company was proving vastly inconvenient. If Kitty did not act with haste, she would forfeit her final opportunity.

"Mary," she called, "I need your help."

Her sister sighed and closed the book in her lap. "With what?"

"Finding a paper that Mamma hid."

Mary's forehead creased. "I cannot conjure any reason she might have to hide papers, but if she did, then she certainly did not mean for us to find them."

Kitty pursed her lips. Stretching the truth might overcome her sister's principles. "That is the trouble. I did manage to read a little, and I think it might be immoral."

"Immoral? What do you mean? Surely you are not accusing our mother of immorality."

"Er...I would not want to repeat it. Perhaps it is best if you judge for yourself." Kitty chewed the corner of her lip. "You are so wise about these matters. I am certain you will know what to do."

This decided Mary, who stood and slipped her book into a voluminous apron pocket.

With the advantage of height, Kitty searched the shelves along the wall near the door, shuffling through the books and scouring the cabinets. Mary moved about behind her, methodically examining the most likely articles of furniture. A solid quarter hour passed in this pursuit before Kitty spun around and flung her arms wide in exasperation.

"I never dreamed finding one measly paper would be this challenging or Mamma so shrewd in hiding it." She pinched her lips in recollection. "The paper was too large for her to tuck into her bosom, and when I returned with her salts, she was in the middle of the room." Kitty moved to stand in the same location, as if that would reveal the hiding place.

Mary said nothing.

Kitty looked to where she knelt by the Bible box, just closing the lid. "Did you find anything in there?"

"The Great Bible and the old Bennet Prayer Book." Mary's answer might have been a trifle hesitant.

"That is obvious." Kitty narrowed her eyes. "You would not lie to me."

"I do not have another minute to waste on these childish games." Mary gained her feet, a scowl marring her features and a condescending tilt to her nose. "I can hardly believe I allowed you to persuade me in the first place. Excuse me."

Kitty mocked Mary's retreating back in silence and glowered at the closing door. It was no more than she should expect from her self-righteous sister, but where could the poem be? She returned to her efforts and was lowering the seat cushion on her mother's armchair some minutes later when Mrs. Bennet entered.

"Why, Kitty," she exclaimed. "What are you doing? I supposed you to be out with Jane and Lizzy, but it is of no consequence. Run find Mary. I want her to try the bonnet we assembled, since she was so insistent on disappearing this morning."

"Mamma, wherever have you been?"

"Never you mind, child." She flicked the backs of both hands toward the door. "Now, along with you."

Kitty wavered, unwilling to leave her mother alone lest she relocate the hidden verses. But when she finally exited, happy humming trailed her down the hall.

*****

Mary slipped into the vestibule and withdrew the folded paper from her apron pocket. Guilt assailed her. She did not lie outright, but still she deceived her sister. Reading only a few words of the verses tucked inside the family Book of Common Prayer was enough to conclude Kitty must not be allowed access again.

Taking care to be quiet, Mary unfolded the half-sheet and read the first two stanzas. Her pulse quickened. It was a love poem in a masculine hand, which meant either Mr. Bingley or Mr. Darcy must have written it. More likely the latter, given the neatness of the writing.

She ought to return it without reading further, and normally she would have, but she was not sure it was appropriate. She read further and her heart began to hammer. By the time she finished, she was certain. Even an engaged couple ought not to be engaging in this sort of word play. She shifted closer to a window and reread the poem in its entirety—only to affirm her original judgment. Indeed. Entirely improper.

"Papa," Mary called as she spun and marched straight to his library door, which stood slightly ajar. When no one answered, she nudged the door open and walked into an empty room. He must be out on estate business. Her eyes fell to the paper again. She found herself involuntarily reading the verses a third time.

"Mary?" Kitty's voice echoed down the hallway.

She cast about for a suitable hideaway, but her sister's footsteps were already in the vestibule.

"Mary, where are you?"

"In here," she answered, fumbling to fold the paper. Her shaking fingers would not cooperate, so she crumpled it into a ball and dropped it in her pocket just as her sister entered.

"What are you doing in Papa's library? But come, Mamma wants you about your bonnet."

Kitty may as well have been speaking another language for all the sense it made to Mary.

"You need not look so stupid. It is only a bonnet."

Mary said nothing, her mouth dry.

Kitty shrugged and turned toward the sitting room, assuming Mary would follow.

Submitting to her mother's ministrations as she manipulated the bonnet on Mary's head was torturous. The wadded paper, which seemed to be burning a hole through her gown, consumed her concentration. Both Kitty and their mother reprimanded her for nonsensical answers, though Mary could not recall what was asked or how she replied.

When at last she was loosed, her relief was excessive. Mary excused herself to the music room, where she could be assured of both solitude and solace. She stood before the pianoforte and looked over the pieces set aside from recent practice: all classical works that would challenge her to improve and exhibit her skill. But today she felt curiously stirred. Such music lacked its customary appeal.

Mary withdrew the poem and flattened it atop the instrument, gently smoothing the wrinkles, mellow white against the rich russet of the mahogany grain. No matter how much she disapproved the content, she was sorry to have spoiled it, but at least it was decipherable. One last time. She examined it, a fingertip tracing the lines, her lips mouthing the words without sound. She studied the paper for several long minutes before refolding and committing it to her pocket. But the cadences continued to pound through her mind in rhythm with her heart.

She reviewed the music again, pushed aside her tidy stack, and dug through Lizzy's jumbled pile until she unearthed a piece that suited. The ballad's arrangement and lyrics were fairly simple, and she found no difficulty playing it on her first attempt. She tried the next song and the next, working her way through Lizzy's repertoire, lost to the music and the passage of time. The air seemed to thicken with the intoxicating scent of roses.

At length, Mary stopped and picked at a chipped ivory key before pulling her hands into her lap and staring at the notes, trying to gauge her feelings and analyze what had changed.

\*\*\*\*\*

Contrary to the opinion of some, a Darcy does not want for patience. But on this day, I was nearing my limits—not that Elizabeth possessed any control over the circumstances. I will not here attempt to enumerate the endless details and engagements attendant on our wedding preparations, but it has afforded me fleeting appreciation for the advantages of eloping to Scotland.

Thus, the afternoon was sufficiently progressed that, in order to keep our planned walk to Elizabeth's favorite Oakham Mount, I requested my coachman leave us at the base and expressed our intention to return on foot to

Longbourn. Having outstripped Bingley and Jane as usual, we summited well before them and came to a halt side-by-side overlooking the Hertfordshire fields and woods. At last I was alone with my beloved. The prospect never fails to please, but on this day, I was more eager to quiz her.

"Elizabeth." I love speaking her name, the most beautiful name in the world. She looked at me with those dancing eyes and that bewitching smile, and I nearly forgot what I was about.

"Yes, Fitzwilliam?"

"Please do not keep me in suspense any longer. Were you able to read my verses?" I was grateful she managed to steal them from the book before Bingley began riffling its pages. His inexplicable behavior was succeeded by an abnormal aloofness all day, despite close quarters in the carriage. I was perplexed by it but preferred not to probe in the ladies' presence.

Elizabeth's answer recalled me. "Yes, I did, though I will admit to wondering why you took such pains to camouflage them."

"I wanted to surprise you. Did I?"

"If you had not informed me, I would never have guessed they were from you."

Uneasiness washed over me. "But did you like the verses?"

Her mouth quirked at the corner. "You know my thoughts on poetry." She referred to a satiric exchange

on the nature of poetry early in our acquaintance, which
was a repeated source of amusement.

But I was not satisfied and turned to fully face her.
"Certainly, but might you not extend more generosity as
they are my verses?"

She arched an eyebrow. "You think I should make an
exception, that they ought not be judged by the same
standard?"

"You may judge whether the alliteration is overdone,
but I think my metaphors will hold up reasonably well."

"That is quite bold of you, my dear, to claim them as
your own." She was teasing me, for which I did not feel
in humor.

"I thought them original," I said, piqued.

She made an unladylike sound somewhere between a
snort and a cough. "I am certain they were when they
were penned, but even you must own that their worth
now is not so much in originality as in familiarity."

I tamped down the irritation beginning to smolder.
How could she treat my verses as if they were tired and
stale phrases when I labored long for love of her? I did
not spill my heart's blood through my pen to have her
dismiss it so casually.

Her hand on my arm calmed me. "Fitzwilliam, please
do not look so peevish."

I am not peevish. I never look peevish.

"Oh, there you go, frowning more gravely, and what
have I said to induce that glower?" She smiled with such
mischievous sweetness when she said this that I could

not resist smiling back. I was struck again, as I have been with frequency in these last weeks, by how well-suited we are and how dearly I need her.

She continued in a more serious tone. "I will always be glad to receive any verses you choose to bestow on me."

I smoothed a thumb across her upturned cheek and sighed. In truth, I was disappointed. This was not the response I expected or for which I hoped, but neither was I ready to abandon the subject. "Will you at least gratify me in this? Were you offended or pleased by my sporting metaphor?"

Her nose wrinkled. "What sporting metaphor?"

"It was not subtle," I objected. "Let me see, 'No nobler field than of your mind, with words and wit we sport in kind.'"

"Oh!" The spark rekindled in her eyes. "Oh, Fitzwilliam, I like that very much, but I would have noted if that were one of the lines."

Trepidation prickled my thoughts. "Have you the verses that we might review them together?"

She rooted about her reticule and produced a square much smaller than the one I had concealed. Unfolded, it was but a thin strip, such as would serve for a bookmark. I did not need to read it.

"Elizabeth, this is not the poem I left for you. Mine was written on a half-sheet with"—I glanced at the several lines—"oh, seven or eight stanzas at least."

She scanned the lines. "These are from a Shakespearean sonnet, but then where are your verses?"

I was thinking the same, dread prickling my neck as I tallied the possibilities with dismay. "You found that in your book?"

"Yes. Jane and I have been reading to each other in turn before we retire, although we did not last night"— her smile was coy—"since our gentlemen departed too late."

Comprehension broke over me, and I chuckled in relief. At best, the poem remained where I hid it. At worst, Jane might have retrieved it in error. While I could not wish to expose my feelings to anyone other than Elizabeth, at least I could trust her elder sister to be tactful and gracious—unlike the remainder of the Bennet family.

"Therein lies the answer." I lifted the paper from her hands. The penmanship was recognizable as Bingley's, though much neater than his routine style, but then he would have made the effort to be legible. "I cannot conceive how Bingley and I happened to coordinate so perfectly."

"What do you mean?"

"This is Bingley's hand. Clearly he hid this intending that your sister would discover it."

"But without knowing you planned to do the same?"

"Precisely. Perhaps you might check the book again when you replace these. If my verses are not there, then it would be prudent to query Jane."

"Of course, but if that is the case, I should like to find a private moment to approach her. She is so modest that I would not wish to cause her embarrassment."

I agreed, and we hurried our return journey. When we descended past Bingley and his betrothed, who were just attaining the outlook, we endeavored to dispel their concern over our speed and encouraged them not to rush.

For the remainder of our walk, Elizabeth invested her energies in cajoling me to disclose more lines from my poem. I taunted her with a single phrase—'sweet as brandy and rich as wine'—and then resisted her further efforts at discovery, though thoroughly delighted by her attempts.

When we entered the house, we both froze in the foyer, transfixed by the stirring music filtering down the stairs. Apart from Elizabeth, Mary is the only other Bennet who plays, but having been subjected to her abilities with abusive regularity, she seemed an improbable candidate.

Elizabeth fairly flew up the stairs.

I followed, eager to discover the enchantress in her lair.

*****

At the edge of vision, Mary noticed the music room door was no longer closed, though she had not heard it open. She pivoted on the stool. The doorway framed Lizzy with Mr. Darcy peering over her shoulder. One hand flew to Mary's mouth to mask a soundless shriek, and her face flamed in discomposure. To see him when he was likely the author of such a poem was too much.

Lizzy advanced, open palm extended until she touched Mary's shoulder. "I did not mean to startle you, but a siren's song beckoned, and I was powerless to resist. I have never heard you play with such feeling. It is really quite moving."

At any other time, the commendation would have fallen warmly on Mary's ears, especially after the many hours Lizzy tutored her at the instrument, but consumed as she was by awkwardness, Mary hardly heard. "Do you know if Papa has returned to his study?"

"I do not know." Lizzy's brows drew together. "We are only just home from our walk."

"You will excuse me." Mary rose and swept past Mr. Darcy, sparing neither word nor glance.

Mr. Darcy's voice reverberated down the stairs, asking Elizabeth what she thought might be amiss, but if it was solicitous, Mary did not pause to credit him, determined as she was to gain her father's library. She knocked on the closed door with insistence and exploded into the room upon his invitation.

"Why, Mary," he exclaimed in mild amazement. "What may I do for you?"

Pulling the inflammatory verses from her pocket, she extended the folded paper to him. "I found this poem in the Bible box when I was aiding Kitty in a search, though I had not an idea of its content. I have speculated that it is from Mr. Darcy to Lizzy, and I would have returned it to her, but as it is in my opinion wholly improper, I thought it best that you should be made aware."

"And not your mother?" There was a funny turn to his countenance.

Mary shook her head.

His laugh was hearty. "Shall we see what little Lizzy is up to?"

Going to her father may not have been the wisest recourse after all. His partiality to Lizzy was unmistakable, and he continually gave her preference over her sisters. If only he would gaze upon Mary with the same loving indulgence.

"It does look a trifle worse for the wear." He unfolded the paper. "Are you certain you have not been rummaging in the dustbin? I assure you I can supply ample reading material. You need not resort to such extremities."

Her mouth turned down. "No, Papa, it was in the Bible box as I said, but I was compelled to conceal it from Kitty."

"I am teasing, child."

Mary loathed it when he did that, jesting in a style she did not grasp but that seemed to invite Lizzy and sometimes Jane to share in his private diversions. He perused the poem, but consciousness of the content made Mary's cheeks heat.

One eyebrow lifted, the other joined it, and his eyes widened. He must be horrified. This justified her actions, and she could not be sorry for misleading Kitty. But then his mouth quirked. He began to smile and murmur an incoherent string of words, "A man after all...besotted...no wonder...oh, Mrs. Bennet."

He set the paper on his desk, shook his head, and chuckled before lifting his eyes to her where she stood gaping in bewilderment. "It is as well you discovered this and not the servants. But come now, you do not look as if you enjoyed it. You are not going to be missish over a few romantic verses are you?"

"Papa!" she cried.

"No, you would not enjoy it, would you." His eyes twinkled with mirth. "Of course you are shocked, my innocent little dove, to have your sensibilities so completely overthrown."

She could not decipher the tenor of his voice and began to suspect he was not in sympathy with her. "But you will do something about it?"

"Yes, yes. I know exactly what to do. And I thank you for bringing this to my attention. When I woke this morning, I never anticipated this day would afford such a degree of entertainment."

Mary knit her brows. There he went again, making light of a serious situation, and she could not approve. He often referred to his son-in-law in the same jocular fashion, even though Mary could never overlook Wickham having lived with Lydia outside of wedlock.

Mary made to leave, but her father hailed her and she paused near the door.

"I would reprimand you for invading personal correspondence, but your conscience is too strict to require it. However, as you are fond of lessons, tell me,"—he tapped the paper against his blotter—"what did you learn from reading this?"

She blushed, a thousand thoughts colliding at once. "I…er…"

"No? Then allow me to rephrase. Did you learn anything of Mr. Darcy?" He added almost under his breath, "As I do not think this Bingley's style."

"Why, I suppose that Mr. Darcy loves Lizzy."

He smiled. "Very good, daughter. Now apply your mind to this. Such verses may not be as improper as you deem them, not from a gentleman to the young lady he is soon to marry." How like her father. When he chose to be serious, he spoke without any sense at all.

Mary was already in the hall when he called after her. "And, if you would, please fetch Mr. Darcy to me."

The short walk from library to sitting room did not suffice to settle the turmoil of thoughts and emotions seething within her.

Mary entered and no one noticed. They rarely did. But when she proceeded to the settee and addressed herself to Mr. Darcy, everyone's attention focused on her. She flushed with mortification.

"My father requests your presence, sir. He is in his library."

Darcy exchanged an unreadable glance with his betrothed and then rose to his full imposing height.

Lizzy lifted an elegant arm bent at the wrist, a playful turn to her countenance. He gave a gallant bow, taking her hand in his, pressing his lips to her fingers, and lingering longer than was necessary. The lavish gesture was unsuited to the setting, but Mary observed them closely. Perhaps true affection bound them after all.

When Darcy turned his dark eyes on Mary with a word of thanks, he seemed different somehow. He was reserved in the extreme when compared to all her family. But was that kindness with which he looked at her?

As he left the room, Lizzy gazed after him. Indeed, her face was alight with joy, her eyes brimming with admiration. She may have even sighed, but the sound was too quiet for Mary to be certain.

"Mary!" Mrs. Bennet's shrill tone made both sisters jump.

Even Jane and Bingley, who occupied the room's far end and whose heads were drawn close in conference, looked up in mild alarm.

"Come here. I would look at you," Mrs. Bennet continued. "Do not just stand there."

Mary moved to her mother's chair, and Mrs. Bennet wrinkled her forehead in appraisal. "Remove your spectacles. Such an unfortunate habit when you are not reading."

Mary did as she was bid.

"Yes, I daresay your color is somewhat improved. There is a rosiness to your cheeks that makes you look not half so plain."

Lizzy cleared her throat with more volume than necessary, but Mrs. Bennet continued pushing at Mary's hair, her eyes following her hands. "And if we arrange your hair in a more becoming style, it will do very nicely."

Both praise and censure fell on dumb ears. Between the poem itself, her father's words, and Lizzy's silent exchange with Mr. Darcy, Mary was too stretched to endure her mother's probing. A tight feeling at the back of her throat presaged tears.

"Mamma," she interrupted, "I am not feeling entirely well. May I be excused to my room to refresh myself?"

"If you must, though why you are always vanishing is beyond me. And you are expected to dinner." Her mother pouted. "I will not have my girls fancying themselves affected and staying above stairs for meals."

As if she were one to talk. Mary quit the room, but not before hearing Lizzy make a derisive noise and Kitty ask, "Whatever is the matter with Mary?"

Mary blinked back the unaccountable tears and paused before her father's study to overhear his lecture to Mr. Darcy. Their lower voices rumbled on the opposite side of the door, but she could not distinguish the words.

If she remained in the sitting room, she might have deduced her father's tactics by Mr. Darcy's reaction. Would he be angry or scornful? In her father's shoes, she would give him quite the tongue lashing, although her father's last statement continued to trouble her. Surely he did not mean to sanction such goings-on? But better to remain in ignorance than to encounter Mr. Darcy before it was necessary. She resumed her progress to the stairs.

On gaining her room, Mary cast herself onto her bed, waves of repressed and unidentified emotion breaking over her and then gradually receding. When the sensation passed, she sat up and giggled. It was so thoroughly uncharacteristic. She did not know what induced her tears, but as she felt improved, it did not merit further consideration.

Mary slipped into the chair at her table and reached for her most precious volumes: the Holy Scriptures, her Prayer Book, and a small journal into which she copied extracts and chronicled those of her musings she judged most memorable. Embossed doves flitted across the journal's Cordovan leather cover, an extravagant gift from her father and reminiscent of the endearment he had bestowed on her. She treasured it.

She opened to a blank page and then grasped the Bible with trembling fingers. The truth of a matter could be judged by this standard. She took a deep breath and began her search.

*****

I was uncertain what to expect when I answered Mr. Bennet's summons, but I was not worried. In the months since he granted us his blessing, I have come to know him better and appreciate him more, especially after dinner when it is only the gentlemen over our libations. He is well-read and quick. Elizabeth is without doubt her father's daughter.

When I entered his library, he gestured for me to close the door and join him in the paired armchairs before his fire. He appeared at leisure, hands folded in his lap, and he studied me in silence. His scrutiny did not disturb me nor did the quiet, but I was on the verge of asking how I might serve when he spoke.

"Are you an aficionado of poetry, Darcy?"

I started. Surely Jane had not taken my poem to her father. "Some verses garner my appreciation, yes," I answered, though not without hesitation. "And you, sir?"

A sardonic note shaded his chuckle. "My passion for it has been renewed of late."

I heard it in his tone. He was toying with me, a habit I find charming in the daughter but often the opposite in the father.

"Mr. Bennet,"—I eyed him with both sternness and respect that he might understand I wished to be serious—"did you invite me to your library to discuss poetry?"

Repentance appeared to reign for a moment before he laughed again. "I did, but I can see you are in no mood to be baited. I will come to the point. It appears you have composed a poem for my Lizzy, a rather heated poem I might add—"

I started to object, but he raised a palm.

"And this poem," he continued, solemnity overtaking his features, "has passed through the hands of Kitty, Mrs. Bennet, and Mary. What say you to that?" I must have blanched, for he added, "You look a trifle pale. Brandy or port, perhaps?"

I shook my head in shock. I needed my wits, not consolation. "An unfortunate development, sir."

"Indeed." He quirked an eyebrow in much the same manner as Elizabeth and examined me once more.

I schooled myself to remain still but felt my discomfort increasing. "May I inquire as to the present whereabouts of my verses?"

"You may." His smile was tight. "They are in my possession, and I will return them to you after we have canvassed several points."

"Please proceed, sir." I wanted to argue that they were my verses, intended for my bride, and no business of his or any other family member, but I held my tongue. After all, this was Elizabeth's father and soon to be my father.

"I think it prudent to acquaint you with the particulars as far as I understand them." He steepled his fingers. "My wife reports that Kitty found the verses in her mother's sewing basket and was, as you might imagine, quite titillated by the reading."

I recalled the lines to mind, but while I acclaimed Elizabeth with all the warmth of a future husband, I would not consider them scintillating. Caught up in this reflection, I nearly overlooked an important detail. "But what were they doing in Mrs. Bennet's sewing basket?"

"I was going to ask you the same."

"I deposited them in a book I know Elizabeth to be reading each evening, with the intention that she would happen upon them before she retired."

"Excellent," he stated, "though not to imply I approve your plan. However, all this tale wanted was a little mystery, and now we have it."

I surmised Jane to be the culprit in relocating the verses, but did not mention my conjecture as there was no reason to expose her—or myself—to the potential for further humiliation.

He continued. "The verses were then transferred to Mrs. Bennet's hands, who also found them very, er, stimulating"—he coughed behind his hand—"and she in turn hid them in the Bible box in a rare show of discretion. Mary, however, proved too ingenious for her and pinched them while assisting Kitty in a hunt for the same."

I sat appalled, contemplating my words in the hands of each Bennet lady.

"Nothing to say, Darcy?" He smirked and then his mouth turned down. "Mary was properly scandalized as she has rigorously avoided any material that borders on indecorous. She has only read 'The Family Shakespeare,' you know."

I frowned in return. "Indecorous seems a bit strong."

He raised both brows and stroked his chin. "Perhaps to men of the world like you and me, but to an innocent and naïve girl…" He let his sentence hang.

"Yes," I allowed, "but they were not written for Miss Mary. I wrote them for Elizabeth, who is—" I stopped. It would not do to say she was not innocent, for she was. We never broached it with openness, but I was aware of her apprehension about marital intimacies and hoped my poetry would go a little way toward easing her. But I could hardly relate this to her father.

"Who is?" he prompted.

"My betrothed," I finished, chagrined by my own inanity.

"And you would do well to remember that, son." He fixed me with a father's severe eye, stunning for its infrequency. "Lizzy is your betrothed. She is not yet your wife. I am not so old that I have forgotten what it is to burn for one's bride, but I would suggest that, should the muse strike again, you retain such verses until your wedding day or thereafter."

I said nothing, containing my annoyance. Was not familial exposure penance enough? His response seemed extreme for my having waxed eloquent on his daughter's charms. I furrowed my brow and recalled the line to which he referred, wherein I described her eyes: 'They hold me fast, I am undone, consumed by fire, a searing sun.' The verses were passionate, yes, but not indecent. Did he not trust me? I am an honorable man. It is true that I await the consummation of our marriage with all eagerness—what bridegroom does not?—but I would in no wise compromise her virtue.

"Very well. If you have nothing further to say, then we understand each other." He clapped his hands together and rose to walk behind his desk. "You have my permission to present this"—he picked up a paper—"to Lizzy. It would not be fair to keep it from her now that most of her family have read it, but I expect you to abide by my request."

I rose as well and waited in silence on the opposite side of his desk.

His penetrating eyes lifted from the paper and focused on me once more.

"Of course." I assented with a curt nod. The circumstances were regrettable in the extreme, but as they could not be undone, I resigned myself.

The tension in his shoulders released and he resumed his habitual mien, which incited my astonishment. My paper recaptured his attention like iron to a magnet. It was deuced awkward. I glanced aside, my gaze falling to a half-dozen volumes in a tidy stack on his desk's edge. I angled my head to read their spines. All poetry.

When I looked at him sharply, he met my eye with his customary satirical twinkle. "Did I not tell you that my interest in poetry has revived?"

"Indeed." I might have chuckled were the circumstances otherwise.

His answering smile hinted at fondness. "Do not mistake me, Darcy. I am not insensible to this affirmation that you love and will love my Lizzy well. They are fine verses and tastefully executed, given their nature. Mary was too overcome, I think, to ever mention it. I will caution Kitty, though I cannot guarantee she will not be invariably silly. I did deem it best for all involved not to disabuse my wife regarding their true authorship. I presume you will agree."

I tried not to choke as he extended the paper to me.

"I do apologize for its tattered state," Bennet said. "Mary admitted to crumpling it in a moment of panic."

I accepted the wrinkled paper and did not waste a moment in reviewing the lines. They were not many, a dark trail on an expanse of white. I was seized by a vision of how Elizabeth's unfettered locks will look curling across a pillow. I shook my head and refocused on the words. Horror gripped me. Surely this was not the poem I had hidden in the book.

# PART III

Mary could not say how much time elapsed since she first seated herself at her desk, but she lingered, hands folded in her lap, feeling much as she did after playing the pianoforte earlier. Notes and references scrawled across her journal, and phrases echoed through her mind: *male and female created He them... a man shall leave his father and his mother, and shall cleave unto his wife: and they shall be one flesh... the woman is the glory of the man... submitting yourselves one to another... husbands, love your wives, even as Christ also loved the church, and gave Himself... a great mystery.*

She even ventured into that most sacrosanct of books, the Song of Solomon, about which she had received emphatic caution and avoided with scrupulousness lest it awaken love before its time. Her astonishment only increased on discovering such verses within the Holy Scriptures. Though much was metaphorical, she inferred enough for her neck and face to heat in response. At least palm trees were not native to England's landscape, as she doubted she would ever view one in the same manner again. To be sure, Solomon's verses made Mr. Darcy's tame by comparison.

Rubbing at a sore spot where the quill chafed her skin, Mary stood and paced about her room. Marriage was an inevitable duty—and in her parents' case, an occasionally unpleasant duty. She had reread the Prayer

Book's matrimonial service, although it was unnecessary, as she was catechized and had attended enough weddings that she could recite the 'causes for which Matrimony was ordained.'

Mary ticked them off on her fingers. Marriage was the proper way to obey the command to be fruitful and multiply. Marriage was the foundation of society's social order, the sphere for the rearing of children. It was for the restraint of lust; did not St. Paul write it was better to marry than to burn? For mutual society, help and comfort, yes, these were all quite practical and logical justifications. She cited these when she disagreed with Lizzy and her father for their criticism of Charlotte Lucas in accepting Mr. Collins.

Mary paused her pacing near the bed, removed her spectacles, and massaged the bridge of her nose then her temples. Did she not reason that Mr. Collins would have made a tolerable husband and, better than that, under her good influence, might have become an agreeable companion? Of course she was his superior in intellect, but she would have encouraged him to read. Guided by her example, he would have been powerless to resist improvement. Would he not?

But now that judgment seemed inadequate, lacking in a critical aspect. She replaced her glasses, moved to the window, and stared into the setting sun. Perhaps there was more to marriage than she previously envisaged. That love and respect for one's spouse might be essential elements, that there might be genuine fulfillment and joy in the meeting of minds, the binding of hearts, and the uniting of bodies was at once frightening and intriguing. She leaned her head against the window frame, the oblique angle making her perspective wavy through the glass. What else could it mean, if marriage was a sacred union and a foretaste in some mystical sense of the great consummation awaiting the end of the age?

Movement on the far side of the window drew her attention to the shrubbery, and she spied Lizzy and Mr. Darcy pausing behind a hedge. From the manner in which he glanced about, he likely thought them unobserved. At any other angle, Mary could not have seen them, but from where she stood, they were just visible in the fading light, the blurry glass circling them like a pinhole. She should retreat, but her recent reflections overruled her scruples and she remained.

Mr. Darcy began speaking, the movements of his mouth augmented now and then with a gesture from his hands.

Lizzy's eyebrows climbed, and she covered her mouth in her habitual manner of stifling laughter. As he continued talking, her amusement faded. She stayed one of his hands in both of hers and shook her head.

He reached into his coat and produced a familiar white square. Mary gasped. Her father must have returned the poem to Mr. Darcy after all.

Lizzy unfolded the paper, and Mary studied her as she read. Her demeanor could only be described as an unguarded expression of pure love. Mr. Darcy also watched in rapt attention, and when Lizzy met his eyes, neither spoke. Their gazes locked in unfathomable intensity.

When Lizzy twined her arms about Mr. Darcy's neck, Mary started in surprise. Mr. Darcy's hands wound around Lizzy's waist, his head inclined toward hers, and they began kissing in a manner the likes of which Mary had never witnessed. She withdrew in discomfiture, her heart pattering.

To be kissed like that by a man who loved her, who would write verses for her, who knew and appreciated all that made her who she was, who would willingly lay down his life for her, awakened a longing she had never known.

Mary crept forward, stealing a glance through the paned glass into the lengthening shadows once more, but they were no longer kissing. Lizzy was nestled in Mr. Darcy's arms, her head cushioned against his chest. His head was bowed, and his lips pressed into her hair. The gloom and the distance made it difficult to ascertain, but it did appear that both their eyes were closed. Yes, to be held thus, to be loved thus would not be at all unwelcome.

*****

Bingley shifted in the carriage and assessed his mute companion as they rumbled toward Netherfield after supper that evening. Darcy had vanished following

Bennet's summons and did not resurface again until dinner, where he appeared with his betrothed on his arm. Both were rather flushed and neither as vocal as normal, which made Elizabeth almost subdued and Darcy essentially mute. From personal experience as well as the manner in which they sat beside one another, Bingley suspected they held hands beneath the table.

Bingley was as pleased for his friend as he was for himself. Being in love was a fine thing. He smiled across the coach's cabin, not that Darcy could see him. But the darkness suited since he needed to broach a sensitive subject and had delayed as long as he dared in introducing it. Horses, hounds, business and even their ladies fair, yes, but he could not recall ever discussing poetry.

"Say, Darce," he spoke in the direction of his friend.

A grunt emanated from the bench opposite.

He hedged for a moment. "Bit of a tricky business, but about the verses you wrote for—"

A bitter laugh cut him short. "What? Not you too."

"Me?"

"Yes. Did you read them?"

"No, but Jane did and she—"

"I presumed as much." Darcy snorted. "Miss Bennet is the least of my concerns, for she is discreet and considerate of her sister."

"You knew?"

"It was easy enough to deduce. But give me the account that we might avoid any further misunderstanding."

Bingley obliged his friend, narrating his conversation with Jane and concluding with an apology. "Alas, neither of us knows what became of the verses after she hid them in her mother's sewing basket. I am sorry, my friend, I tried."

"And I thank you. Would it were so easy." The depth of Darcy's sigh made his regret palpable. "I owe you an explanation in turn. Elizabeth unwittingly carried away and read your verses before she found opportunity to replace them. Since she and Jane have been reading the same book, the location is not a mystery, but the coincidence of our timing borders on the extraordinary—or the perverse."

"Shall I warn you next time I hide verses for Jane?" Bingley spoke half in jest.

"No need." Darcy's tone was wry. "I am cured of my belief in a romantic element to surprise."

Bingley waited, his hearing full of creaking wood and wheels on the lane, but his friend did not seem inclined to say more. "What did happen, if I may ask?"

"Not a story you want to hear, nor I to relate."

"That will never do. Come, man, out with it."

Bingley nearly despaired of an answer, but Darcy began to speak. "It all began when I composed two poems."

"Two?"

"What can I say? Elizabeth inspires me." The gentle appreciation in his tone succumbed to sarcasm as he recounted the misadventures of his romantic poetry. "In short, the blasted poem traveled through every Bennet's hands, save her for whom it was written, before finding its way back to me."

"Bad luck that, on both fronts." But Bingley could not check himself and a mirthful sound escaped. "No wonder the family behaved so oddly this evening."

"Do not think on it." Darcy groaned. "You will have nightmares."

"No, truly, did you not notice how Kitty and Mary were nearly swooning over you?"

"I observed it."

"And when Mary petitioned her mother for another dress fitting before the wedding, I thought Mr. Bennet would die of apoplexy from curbing his laughter."

Darcy did not comment, and Bingley wished he could see his face.

Bingley cleared his throat. "Neither you nor Elizabeth appeared entirely guileless in that exchange."

"Have I ever told you that you are altogether too sanguine?" Darcy had with some frequency and in the same acerbic tone, but it did not deter Bingley. However he might disclaim, Darcy appreciated his optimism.

"At least Mrs. Bennet was preoccupied this evening and left us to our devices more than is her wont. She may as well have been in Mr. Bennet's pocket for all she kept so close to him—not that he seemed to mind."

Bingley's supposition of the morning struck him with the additional force of Darcy's revelations. "Oh, this is rich—you do not suppose your verses are why the senior Bennets, er…"

Only road noise answered him.

Bingley nevertheless vouchsafed a satisfied chuckle. "Cheer up, old man. Your trials were not without effect. Besides, you have my gratitude for inspiring Jane to bestow her favors on me, and after all this, I certainly hope you achieved your desired result."

"Any credit is due exclusively to yourself, Bingley, not my mislaid words." Darcy's assertion was earnest and firm. "They only fanned a flame that was already bright."

Bingley smiled toward the indistinct silhouette. What his friend said was true. When they returned from their walk that afternoon, Jane searched the book again, and both were relieved to find his lines from the sonnet. The instant smile and flush that graced her features made plain her delight. Since they were chaperoned in the sitting room, she was unable to thank him by more than squeezing his hand and gazing at him meaningfully with her limpid brown eyes, but he did perceive she was genuinely moved by his effort.

"Any chance I may read these tantalizing verses, Darcy?"

"I am afraid not, and you must understand why."

"Naturally. You are not offended that I asked?"

"No. I doubt this will be either the first or the last time such private matters are exposed between us."

Bingley laughed. "No doubt."

A thoughtful pause ensued.

When Darcy spoke again, his voice resonated with sentiment. "But I cannot think of a man I would rather have for my brother."

\*\*\*\*\*

In the candlelight, auburn ripples chased each long, smooth stroke through Lizzy's shiny brunette waves. Jane's hand wielded the brush with mechanical repetition, her mind preoccupied with the accounts they traded regarding Darcy's wayward poem. They had forsaken the fateful book for the second night in a row.

"I still can scarce believe it," Jane said. "But, oh, poor Mr. Darcy—how he must have felt it."

"Yes, it is true, although I think you may feel it more than he." Lizzy chuckled. "He can see the absurdity of the whole, though it pains him yet."

"Oh, no, it is positively mortifying." Jane's cheeks warmed, confirmed by a peek at the mirror over Lizzy's head.

"Do not worry. I have enough wisdom to postpone my teasing a little, but I do predict we will share many a laugh. This day belongs to the infamy of Bennet and Darcy history."

Jane's sympathies were too full to encompass humor. "And, Mary, dear innocent Mary, I cannot imagine how troubled she must be."

"On the contrary," Lizzy said with a light laugh, "she is half in love with Fitzwilliam already."

"Please do not joke about such a thing."

"You think I am jesting?" Her sister rotated on the stool, faced Jane, and took the brush from her hand to set it on the vanity. "She came to me earlier to apologize, and after that was done, we had our first heart to heart conversation that I can recall. She does not understand, not really, not yet, what it means to give oneself in loving another, but the entire ordeal humbled her, I think, helped her to see how much she does not know. That cannot be all bad."

"No," conceded Jane, though still somewhat shocked and not quite persuaded.

"I am not certain I can say the same for Kitty," Lizzy said with a rueful shake of her head. "Her enthusiasm to visit Pemberley has trebled, but she will probably turn the house inside out in a quest for provocative poetry."

"Surely not. She must have learned her lesson."

"She is not you. But at least Newcastle and the Wickhams have been overshadowed, and with Georgiana's refined influence, I do not think Kitty can help but improve."

"Oh, Lizzy, what you have endured. First Mary, then Kitty and now me, all plaguing you about your verses. I am so sorry."

"It has been quite the parade." She giggled. "Of course, Kitty did not come to apologize but to entreat me to show them to her. Can you imagine?"

Jane could not. "I hope you have hidden them well."

Lizzy beamed, her eyes twinkling. "They are in the safest place conceivable. In fact, I told Kitty outright in order to put an end to any snooping and to silence her on the subject."

"You did not."

Lizzy sobered. "After Fitzwilliam explained the affair, he offered the verses to me and I declined."

"You what?" Jane could not mask her disbelief.

"He wrote them for our first night as husband and wife." Lizzy's expression was poignant. "For me to read them now, only because everyone else has? It would not be the same. It is such a precious gift, and I wanted to honor him."

Jane beheld her sister in wonder. Already she was maturing under her betrothed's influence. Lizzy had always been perceptive and compassionate, but this reflected a higher degree of discernment and devotion.

Jane took Lizzy's face between her hands and pressed a fond kiss to her forehead. "I am so very proud of you."

"Do not be too proud." Lizzy laughed again. "I am not sure I would have had the fortitude if he did not present the correct verses in their place."

"You mean the ones he intended to give you all along?"

"Yes." Her cheeks pinked, and she ducked her head in uncharacteristic diffidence. "If you would like to read them, I would not mind."

"No, no." Jane shook her head. "I think I have had more than my share of your verses. But it does pain me to know that I have read what you have not."

Lizzy reached to grasp her sister's hands, her expression earnest. "Do not trouble yourself so. He wrote them for me, for our wedding, and he is keeping them until then. You have spoilt nothing." Her tone grew wheedling. "Are you certain you do not want to read the others?"

Lizzy's dark eyes glittered in the candle's glow, her thick, loose mane tumbling down her back. Regular compliments underscored Jane's beauty, but the second eldest Bennet sister wore a crown of glory. How often had Jane combed those lustrous tresses? But their nighttime routine approached its end. Within a fortnight, they would be divided by miles, their hair brushed by their respective maids, and their husbands... she colored at the thought. If Lizzy wished to share her verses, Jane would not deny her. So few opportunities for cherished confidences remained.

Jane exhaled a bittersweet sigh. "Very well, let us see these momentous verses."

Lizzy sprang up, taking the candle in one hand and grabbing Jane with the other, nearly dragging her across the room in her eagerness. When they were seated on the bed, their nightdresses and wraps pooled about their knees in a froth of white linen, Lizzy reached under her pillow and withdrew a neatly folded paper looking very much like the one Jane had found early that morning.

Jane opened it slowly and read the lines. Lizzy's chin settled on her shoulder as she followed along.


No gladder sound upon my ear
      than your merry laugh, light and clear.
I've tuned my heart to sing with yours
      the poetry where our love soars:

No nobler field than of your mind,
      with words and wit we sport in kind,
But finer still, your heart and soul
      awash in joy, I am made whole.

No crashing wave upon the rocks
      compares to your cascading locks,
Shining, swirling, they beckon me
      to dive within and plumb their sea.

No brighter aspect than your eyes,
      in darkest night, my starry skies;
They hold me fast, I am undone,
      consumed by fire, a searing sun.

No more potent taste have I known
      than of your lips upon my own,

Sweet as brandy and rich as wine;
    sustain me, O beloved mine.

No costly perfume can compete
    with your pure scent; I am replete.
More fragrant than exotic spice:
    you ravish me—enthralled, enticed.

No smoother skin than of your face
    and every line I wait to trace,
To touch, embrace, and worship thee:
    a sacrament of unity.

No greater promise will I make
    in covenant; this vow I'll take:
To have, to hold, my honored wife,
    to give you all, my love, my life.

They lingered in profound silence, the paper resting in Jane's lap. The lines stirred her and limned her eyes with moisture. She crooked an arm upward, cupped her palm against her sister's head, still quiescent on her shoulder, and then stroked her silky hair. Jane could not see her face, but she did not need to.

"Oh, how he loves you, Lizzy. How he loves you."

\*\*\*\*\*

Alone in my chambers at Netherfield and dressed for sleep, I placed the taper next to my writing table on the desk. My poem reposed on the blotter, appearing innocuous enough, despite having provoked the fracas at Longbourn. I recalled that dreadful moment in Mr. Bennet's study when I realized what I had done. He again recommended port, and this time I accepted.

How I concealed the incorrect verses within Elizabeth's book, I will never know, except that I did so in a moment of distraction, an aberration to my normal behavior, but for which I have developed a recent proclivity when thinking about or within my beloved's presence. I shake my head now in amusement. None other has her capacity to completely undo me.

When I explained my blunder to her father, he apprehended the humor, though I could not—not then. He was nearly as glad as I to redeem my dignity, professing that while my sentiment did not astonish, my judgment in timing did. This resolved, I begged use of a horse, having come in my carriage to escort the ladies on their errands, departed at once for Netherfield to retrieve the proper poem, and returned well within the hour. With some reluctance, yet convinced it was the appropriate course, I conveyed my willingness to present this second set of verses to Bennet for his approval, but he was unconcerned, his trust having been restored. If he was curious, he gave no indication.

In this I exult, I could have answered Bingley's assertion in the affirmative: I did achieve my desired result. Other consequences aside, I did not miss the irony that both he and Bennet benefited at my expense. But they were equally shortsighted if they thought I composed the lines in order to obtain something from Elizabeth. Yes, we shared an unforgettable kiss, but I wrote the verses to bring her joy, to give her pleasure, to communicate to her how much I love her and long for her. I wanted nothing from her but that she might be assured of my deepest affections.

The heartfelt emotion that stole over her face as she read delineated my success. It started in her eyes and overtook every feature, softening her brow, bowing her mouth like the first rays of dawn melting the frost-clad earth. Her countenance shone with my love and her love, mingled there as she beheld me with such tenderness and adoration as would dim the sun.

Those verses are secure in her hands. I smile to envision her perusing them that they may whisper my love in the thin place between waking and sleeping.

As for the other, the poem before me is considerably creased and worn. I could transcribe it onto a clean sheet, but it is yet readable and somehow the more prized for having been given and returned. It speaks to me of Elizabeth's nobility, of her love and esteem, that she would wish to uphold my original intention. I am marrying the wisest and worthiest of women.

I lift the paper from the table, fold it with care, and move to my jewel case atop the bureau, where I asked that it be left. I slide the small, crinkled rectangle along the blue velvet lining and under the tidy rows of cravat pins and fobs. A caution in the morning to my valet, who is discretion personified, and it will remain untouched. The hinges snap closed with gentle pressure.

I rest my hand atop the lid as I contemplate the words within, so many flower bulbs sleeping the winter dreams of imminent spring. After my account and Elizabeth's deferral, neither of us has mentioned it again, nor will we, I think, not before we are wed. I dare not imagine more. And so it waits and I wait, a promise not yet made, a hope not yet fulfilled, until the day I will lead her into Eden unashamed.

# EPILOGUE

Elizabeth woke and blinked into the unfamiliar dimness. What was this incongruous heat when she expected vapor made visible and toes nearly frozen by the morning's cold? She started to roll away from the fire, but an odd weight immobilized her, and she remembered.

Within his slumbering embrace, she was sheltered, protected, adored. His chest warmed her back, the flame that had awakened her. His slow, even breath caressed her neck. His broad hand covered her own, his fingers intertwined with hers, pressing into the ring with which he vowed himself only yesterday. His voice, solemn and steady, reverberated in her memory: *with this ring I thee wed, with my body I thee worship, and with all my worldly goods I thee endow.*

As surely as they covenanted with each other before God and His church, they were joined now, inseparably, inextricably, in a bond that only death could dissolve. She recalled how they gave themselves to one another, withholding nothing. Apprehension yielded to awe, embarrassment to elation, and uncertainty to glorious union. *Flesh of my flesh, bone of my bones, become one.* It was an exquisite paradox, at once timid and bold, tender and untamed, surrendered and triumphant.

Elizabeth lay in prolonged awareness, luxuriating in his nearness and alert to the novelty of every sensation.

Fatigue made her sluggish, but when further sleep eluded her, she slipped from under his arm and from between the linens. He shifted but did not rouse. She retrieved her dressing gown and wrapped herself against the chill. She padded about their bedchamber, hunting by the faint light seeping from around the edges of the draperies until she found the object of her search where it had fallen, abandoned.

Crossing to the window, she parted the curtains a sliver. Morning sun illuminated the article in her hand. Of all his wedding presents, she treasured most this wrinkled half-sheet of foolscap. Though the ink was smeared in several places, she read again as he first had read to her before they were lost to wonder and mystery.

> Through your eyes so bright and fine
> Calls soul to soul, mind to mind
> In the joining of our hands
> The end of sorrow
>
> Under the veil of your hair
> Along your curves, lithe and fair
> Into Eden unashamed
> I long to follow
>
> In the parting of your lips
> In your every swell and dip
> In the valley beautiful
> Is heaven borrowed

In the wonder of this night
The agony of delight
By a holy mystery
We will be swallowed

In the giving of my life
In the loving of my wife
In the union of our hearts
All our tomorrows

Hearing movement, Elizabeth glanced over her shoulder. Diffused sunlight slanted across the bed, and her eyes roved over him with the same reverent love as had her hands. She marveled at the contented planes of his face, the errant locks of his hair, and the captivating strength of his form. His words echoed in her ears and pounded in her heart. He was her husband now. Fitzwilliam Darcy, her beloved, her friend.

# AFTERWORD

My goal is to write the type of fiction I like to read—imaginative, wholesome, romantic, and moving—and to convey it through prose that echoes with poetic sensibility. If I can achieve that, then it will be a fitting tribute to Jane Austen, whose characters and plot we so liberally borrow. More importantly, it will be honoring to God, to whom I owe both gratitude for the gift of words and allegiance in its stewardship.

The geneses of the stories included in this volume are briefly explained below. If they made you smile or laugh or touched your heart, please consider letting others know by leaving a review. You can also contact me through my website www.reneebeyea.com, Goodreads, or Facebook (www.facebook.com/reneebeyea) author pages. I'd love to hear from you!

Yours, Renée Beyea

**Conception**: The two-hundredth anniversary of *Pride & Prejudice*'s publication was celebrated on 28 January 2013. A reader at Derbyshire Writers' Guild suggested authors might commemorate the anniversary by writing stories on the theme. This poem was my contribution.

**Words in the Wind**: *A trail of mysterious words tracks Elizabeth to the Meryton graveyard, where she has an unexpected encounter with Mr. Darcy.*

Derbyshire Writers' Guild holds an annual writing challenge denoted by the improbable name JAOctGoHoNo (Jane Austen October Gothic Horror Nonsense). Writers are given until 31 October to produce a story incorporating the theme presented at the beginning of the month.

Due to life circumstances, I had taken off more than a year from writing, but my family gave me writing time for my birthday—which happens to be in October. I pounded out the initial 8,000 word draft in a single eight hour run that started after I put my sons to bed and ended at 3 a.m. Although I invested many times those hours in revisions, I do wish I could always write so fast.

In 2014, the theme was "ten"—hence the recurrence of ten throughout the piece and my choice for the opening quote, "...he scarcely spoke ten words to her." The quote also situates the beginning of the story, which isn't fully explained until the first extract from Darcy's journal. The very night he resolved not to speak to

Elizabeth was also the night he inscribed those life-altering words in his journal. I leave the mystery of the copyist to the reader to determine, but along with Darcy, I credit the hand of Providence.

**A Fine Stout Love or The Efficacy of Poetry**: *When Darcy is assailed by an errant and rather evocative specimen of poetry lurking in Longbourn's drive, Elizabeth's verses are unexpectedly tested for their efficacy.*

I've always had a fondness for Darcy and Elizabeth's satiric little exchange about poetry's effectiveness. I don't think Jane Austen intended their banter to be taken seriously. But what if one of them composed a verse about the other? Whose theory would it support: Darcy's reference to the common understanding that poetry feeds love, or Elizabeth's contention that poetry only nurtures a love that's strong already? According to this story, they're both correct.

Readers enjoyed Elizabeth's Account, originally titled *On the Efficacy of Poetry*, but were clamoring to know what she wrote that would evoke such a response in Darcy. In her account, it wasn't necessary to actually compose the poem, only to imagine it in vague terms. Loving to craft poetry as I do, this was a challenge I couldn't resist. Add to that the fun of shifting to Darcy's point of view in order to tell his version of the same tale and this pair of stories has become indivisible.

**Neither Slumber Nor Sleep**: *Too weary to continue shopping for her sister's wedding, Elizabeth seeks respite in a nearby church, but her rest is disrupted by an outrageous occurrence.*

It's not uncommon for me to launch a story based on a single scene. An image presents itself, and then I puzzle out what happened before and after. This story started with Darcy and Elizabeth trapped beneath a collapsed bench. Even if Elizabeth could see the humor, it would have been mortifying for both, especially the dignified Darcy. So I decided to tell the story of the bench, how they came to be there, and what resulted.

While I intended the title to suggest multiple connotations, it is taken from Psalm 121—"he that keepeth Israel shall neither slumber nor sleep." This was the scripture reference inscribed on the faded brass plate. I imagine Darcy acquiring the actual plate and affixing it to a new bench overlooking Pemberley. The more romantic may contend he removed the actual mound of kindling from the church garden and commissioned it rebuilt. Either way, he would have chosen the location— as described in the story's initial paragraph—based on the psalm's opening line, "I will lift up mine eyes unto the hills, from whence cometh my help."

**Gold, All Gold**: *Darcy rescues Elizabeth in the Netherfield woods, but all is not as it seems.*

This is another story that launched from a single scene. For a while, I'd had this strange, inexplicable vision of a bronzed Darcy and Elizabeth standing before a brass sea. I was fascinated and, since speculative fiction is another favorite genre, set out to convey the wonder of that golden realm and to tell the story of why they were there. At the time, I was also in the middle of a tedious non-writing project and, dare I confess, reveled in the excuse for creative procrastination. I leave it to the reader to decide how the dreams within dreams operate.

**Eden Unashamed**: *When Darcy's attempt to surprise Elizabeth with a love poem goes terribly awry, no member of the Bennet family escapes its effects.*

This story came to me while standing in line at the grocery. I noted down the main plot movements on the reverse of my shopping list, then furiously scribbled further thoughts in the parking lot while the ice cream melted. Few of my short stories involve sub-plots, but this one does. In resolving the mystery of Darcy's wayward love poem, we also witness the awakening of Miss Mary Bennet.

Rather than imposing the distraction of footnotes on this story, I have listed references here in order of allusion (King James Version for authenticity): Proverbs 25:11; Genesis 1:27, 2:24; 1 Corinthians 11:7; Ephesians 5:21, 25, 32; Song of Solomon 2:7, 7:7-9; Genesis 1:22; *Book of Common Prayer* 1662, Everyman's Library, pp. 299-307; 1 Corinthians 7:9; Revelation 21:1-4; Genesis 2:23; Song of Solomon 5:16. The title is from Genesis 2:25.

# ACKNOWLEDGMENTS

Debut books, even short story collections, are notorious for their long lists of acknowledgements, and mine is no exception. How else does an author acknowledge the many who have played a role in achieving this longed-for culmination?

First, I dedicate this book in loving memory of Karisa Bennett, my childhood best friend and truly the sister of my heart. She will always be the Lizzy to my Jane— sunny and charming, quirky and full of joy. The countless hours we spent reading novels, watching *The Princess Bride*, singing lyrics from *The Sound of Music* and *My Fair Lady*, and planning romances for our horses became seeds for the tales I write. I smile to picture you, dear sweet friend, arrived now at the heart of the Greatest Romance ever told, and I look forward to joining you at the Lamb's wedding feast.

I also wish to express sincere gratitude to my parents, Jim and Marietta, and my brother, Jeon, for a lifetime of unstinting support; to my high school English teachers and college professors, who taught me word craft; to Rebecca, who applauded my early efforts and nurtured my writing dream for twenty-two years; and to all the family and friends who happily indulged my poetry and stories from secondary through graduate school and beyond.

To the members of Derbyshire Writers' Guild, an online Jane Austen Fan Fiction community, without whose inspiration and readership I would never have dreamed these stories; to my Christian Writers' Guild mentor, for refreshing my writer's memory after a fifteen year hiatus and teaching me new skills; to fellow JAFF writers, especially Ginger Monette for her immeasurable help, advice, and encouragement; to Sharon, proofreader par excellence; and to Roseanna White Designs for the exquisite covers that truly 'capture my words.'

To Hannah, Tamara, and Erin, who cared for my boys when I needed to work in the office; to Dick and Betty, who make dreams come true; to my sons, for their patience with my unceasing stints at the computer; and most especially to my husband, Rick, and partner in the creative process, for brainstorming and listening, believing and loving.

I give thanks to the Lord for each of you.
Soli Deo Gloria.

PRIDE & PREJUDICE
PETITE TALES
2

# WHAT *Love* MAY COME

*and other stories*

## Renée Beyea

**COMING WINTER 2016**

# What Love May Come and Other Stories

Pride & Prejudice Petite Tales, Volume 2

Join Elizabeth Bennet and Fitzwilliam Darcy as they discover the hope of second chances and the triumph of joy over sorrow in this novella-length story collection.

- Three years after the death of his wife, Darcy visits Longbourn to reminisce. Will he find laughter and maybe even love once more?

- While extended family celebrates, Elizabeth is privately mourning a miscarriage. Will attending a Christmas service bring solace to her grief?

- A shocking secret threatens Darcy and Elizabeth's reunion twenty-five years after their Hunsford debacle. Can they surmount their pasts to rekindle their love?

- After reliving sublime moments in his marriage, Darcy faces the prospect of life without Elizabeth. How will he meet his future?

Like fine dark chocolate, these poignant period shorts will moisten the eye and stir the heart, but their rich taste will linger long after they are finished.

*If you would like to receive occasional emails about release dates and other new stories, please sign up at www.reneebeyea.com.*

## ABOUT THE AUTHOR

Renée Beyea holds an undergraduate writing degree
from Taylor University and a Master of Divinity from
Fuller Seminary. She serves as full-time wife, mother to
two sons, and ministry partner with her husband, an
Anglican priest and chaplain. Her free time is devoted to
crafting stories and composing poetry that delight the
senses and touch the soul.

www.reneebeyea.com
www.facebook.com/reneebeyea